PRAISE FOR

HEART OF EARTH

Book One of

The Changing Hearts of Ixdahan Daherek

"This fun YA sci-fi novel — with well-rounded characters, interesting premise, and lighthearted dialogue — will delight readers of every age. The sci-fi aspects are entertaining and fun, and the character growth will keep the attention of those who don't typically read the genre."

— Paige Van De Winkle, *Foreword Reviews*

"An alien criminal exiled to Earth with dire — and hilarious — consequences. An irresistible blend of wonky science and heartfelt storytelling. Holding it all together is Laporta's spot-on portrayal of life as a teen. [A] fabulous read!"

— *Kirkus Reviews*

"When I finished reading the tenth page of Heart of Earth I knew the novel was going to take me on a sci-fi adventure I would remember and talk about…. I highly recommend this novel for anyone who is looking to satisfy their cravings for good sci-fi or just plain good reading. Five Stars!"

— Sherrod M. Wall (Author, *From Heaven to Earth*)

"It's infused with subtle humor.... I actually got a clutch in my throat towards the end.... Really good, stand-alone YA sci-fi with potential for sequels. Recommended!"

— K. A. Krisko (Author, *Stolen*)

"A funny, charming, and down-right dorky tale that blends sci-fi and YA together seamlessly. It's the kind of book I ate up like candy through middle and high school ... and it reminded me how much *fun* YA could be.... The characters are charming and the writing is exquisite.... We need more storytellers like Laporta!"

— Tay Laroi, *Truth about Books* blog

THE CHANGING HEARTS OF IXDAHAN DAHEREK

BOOK ONE
HEART OF EARTH

MARK LAPORTA

MARK LAPORTA

HEART OF EARTH

MARK LAPORTA is a dreamer, a humanist and science enthusiast, who sees the light in the dark, the noise in the silence and the humor in just about everything. Aside from *almost* knowing French, he's also a composer, with an ear to the ground for a slightly saner future. He lives in New York City with his wife and son.

THE CHANGING HEARTS
OF IXDAHAN DAHEREK

BOOK ONE

HEART OF EARTH

Chickadee Prince Books
New York

For Janet and Alex

CHAPTER ONE

"Has to be a way out," rasped the solitary prisoner. Tapping the hyperdimensional synapses of the Galactic Array, he scanned the few data clusters still open to his mind. If he dug through the court transcript, he might find a flaw in the Prosecution's case.

Too bad he'd skipped the last six sessions of AP Criminal Law; he could have *used* some legal advice, even his own.

"Hopeless," the prisoner muttered, as despair seeped into every cell of his body. At 1,000 pages, the transcript was a twisting labyrinth of slick legal jargon.

Better to look away.

Trouble was, with no distractions, he had nowhere to hide from his misery: stuck in a Snaldrialooran transmog chamber, caught between the *chahalm drohkaar* he knew and the hideous creature he'd see in the mirror tomorrow. His name was Ixdahan Daherek and, when he wasn't in a coma, he was angry as a Glalifrontian guard dog between meals.

Not that you could blame him. In spite of spine-wracking pain, he couldn't even writhe; there wasn't enough left of his eight blue-gray tentacles for more than an anemic wriggle. Between muscle spasms, the humiliation of it stung hard.

Lucky for Ixdahan, his mind had been safely uploaded to the ship's core processors. Yet the only thing on his mind at the moment were the court records, and they were seriously depressing. For his single act of treason, he'd been exiled to *Hathreahdahnaar*, a planet whose only sentient species was a tribe of ape-descended, gas-breathing bipeds.

"Barely a Level 2 civilization!" Ixdahan wailed into the semi-transparent transmog chamber that was, for now, inflicting a slightly less horrific form of agony on his three tri-cameral hearts.

And to think his ordeal had begun with a single file, downloaded illegally from the Ministry of Defense and sent off to the Vrukaari embassy. But in Ixdahan's mind, his only fault had been following family tradition.

He'd never bothered himself with interstellar politics before, unlike his father, Pertahru, or Thahaga Daherek, his great Aunt. The diplomatic corps? Way too much responsibility. But in this case, the consequences had seemed too remote to burden his conscience. What did rumors of Vrukaari atrocities on distant worlds matter to him?

What *had* mattered were the weeks of planning to steal Father's security codes, then the endless waiting — until the stupid old *pilaarn* went off-world on a diplomatic mission. Risky? Why worry about the risks, when the payoff included thousands of credits and entrée into the subculture of foreign intrigue? And hadn't he been forced into action, the moment Father had cut his allowance in half?

"Merchant ships! Holochambers! Game rooms!" the Scion of L'ahn-Singa Province had thundered. "You're *supposed* to be preparing yourself for service to the Homeworld."

Ixdahan had kept silent, knowing nothing he could say would make the slightest dent in Father's rage.

"Listen carefully," Pertahru had sneered, "I refuse to finance your degenerate behavior. If you insist on wasting your life, you'll have to become more resourceful!"

Well, if selling state secrets wasn't being resourceful, nothing was. And what harm would it do? That gaggle of Vrukaari warlords could barely stop drooling, let alone build a functioning transmog device.

Besides, he'd told himself, if Ambassador Ghaar hadn't used Ixdahan, she would have found another agent. And what other agent was more deserving of her cold, hard credit tiles than the only remaining heir to House Daherek?

Yet now, it was Ixdahan who was bound for exile. No other agent had seen his rank and privilege shrunk to the three instances of *khaldahrn drolghar*, or "personal preference."

The ship's chronograph chimed and the teenage son of Snaldrialoor's most honored diplomat attempted to shake his head. The journey was already one-third over and he still hadn't formulated an escape plan. Not that there weren't obstacles.

"Can't move," he grumbled, unable to close his eyes or scratch the itch he felt ... somewhere ... it wasn't at all clear. For while the onboard navigation system was busy reassigning the ship's quantum signature, the transmog chamber continued to remap Ixdahan's genome with brutal efficiency.

Taking a closer look at his case files, Ixdahan learned that the court-mandated transmog process included a full complement of adaptive memories and an integrated array of neuro-muscular skills suitable to his new environment. Maybe that would make his new surroundings a bit less terrifying — and maybe it wouldn't.

Desperate for any shred of comfort, he combed the court documents and discovered this: His planet of exile boasted two large oceans of liquid hydrogen oxide. Ironically, with his new body, he'd need a special breathing apparatus to explore them.

Yet for all he knew, he'd never get near Earth's oceans. Instead of roaming free, Ixdahan would be supervised by a pair of robotic caretakers, "programmed to fulfill all necessary parental functions."

Sacred Mentality of the Dark Voids, how far he had fallen!

Struggling against drug-induced sleep, Ixdahan relived the day he was captured. He saw himself fretting in the anteroom of the Interstellar Consortium's Chamber of Entities, his tentacled torso darting through the surrounding ocean of liquid methane, while Pertahru glared at him from a 3-meter square monitor mounted on the far wall.

At minus 161.6° Celsius, the oceans of Snaldrialoor would have been deathly cold to humans. But to Ixdahan, squirming in his 2,000-year-old ceremonial armor, the anteroom had felt a shade too hot.

Finally, the Chamber's majestic ovoid portal had swung open and Ixdahan had swirled over to Speaker's Podium — determined to stand trial with dignity.

Yet his scheduled meeting with Supreme Magistrate Grellahnk Kolorytha was in no sense a trial. Before Ixdahan had drawn his next breath, a squadron of Consortium militia had stripped off his ceremonial armor, knocked him unconscious and hustled him off to a squat, smelly cell 300 meters down. After hours of waiting, and a cursory interrogation by a low-level Intelligence operative, he'd been dragged out again, shoved into a transmog chamber and flung off to space.

Now, as his eyes blinked open, the starspanner's final spatio-temporal leap brought Ixdahan to the outer edges of the newly discovered solar system. Coughing, he watched the last drops of liquid methane evaporate in the hot transmog chamber and ... What? ... *Sacred*.... He was being poisoned by a gaseous mixture of oxygen, nitrogen and argon!

Yet his new alien body welcomed the change with an involuntary shiver of sensual pleasure. Ashamed, his transmogged hearts nearly choked with rage. What right did the Consortium have to humiliate him, force him to feel ... sensations ... that....

He should resist. He should ... regain....

But his mind was not his own. And as the starspanner began the final leg of its journey, Ixdahan Daherek, teenage intergalactic criminal, was lost in an alien tropical paradise — a world woven from sensor data fed directly into his startled cerebral cortex.

Soon, a delicious creature seemed to appear before him, her golden hair blowing in the breeze beside a hydrogen oxide sea. Though he knew that she was no more than the ghost of an implanted memory, he found her no less irresistible. As he lapsed into a coma for the final stages of the transmog process, Ixdahan realized he was hopelessly in love.

CHAPTER TWO

Lena Gabrilowicz looked out over the ocean at Felicity Bay and breathed deep in the salty air. Though she'd visited the coast every summer for her entire life, the way the water shimmered in the early evening never failed to sooth her soul. She could watch the light flicker for hours, hear the gulls squawk in the distance and listen to the slap of wave against hull until she was fast asleep, collapsed on the deck with no thought of tomorrow.

Not wanting to stress herself, Lena had dropped anchor only 200 yards offshore—just far enough to feel the wide ocean's pull at her keel. How great it would be to stay out on the water alone forever, with no one to lay a giant guilt trip on her whenever she wanted a little quiet time.

"Go, get out and have fun with the other kids," Dad kept nagging, "you only get so many weeks of vacation before you have to hit the books again."

Oh, yeah, "The Books," one more item on her list of Things I Never Want to Hear Again. But when your dad's a high school History teacher and your mom … well, Lena didn't want to think about Mom right now. It would have spoiled the mood.

But as the water called out to Lena again, it tugged on the memory of her last summer with Mom four years ago. In the yellow light bouncing off the bay, Lena's fingers fidgeted with the silver Star of David necklace around her neck. It had been a twelfth birthday present from Mom, and was now one of the few tangible links Lena had to her past.

"Hey, your dad's got some beers in the fridge," yelled Callie Ann from inside the cabin.

So much for solitude. Not that Lena could complain. She was lucky to be out on the water at all. That is, it had seemed like luck at first. Bored out of her mind, she'd asked Dad if she could take the cat boat cruiser out, never expecting him to say yes—and never guessing he'd toss her the marina keys in one fluid motion. Usually, Dad was kind of a klutz, but not tonight. Tonight he had the reflexes of a cheetah.

"Just don't go out alone," he'd said, resting his rope-rough hands on her shoulders.

Lena was so thrilled she was half way to Callie Ann's beach house before it hit her. Dad had a date with that florist, Rhea Silber. He'd invited her over for dinner and everything.

"So, what's the deal?" called Callie Ann, "should I pop a couple open?"

"Don't ... even ... think ... about ... it!" shouted Lena. She'd get grounded for sure, out here on the bay, where there was nothing to do as it was, and 100 times less to do if you couldn't even go out of the house.

"Loser," said Callie Ann, hauling herself out of the cabin.

"Come on," said Lena, "check out the view. It'll be sunset soon."

"Forget it," said Callie Ann, slipping off her sneakers. "I'm swimming to shore. You can snooze out here all you want."

Before Lena had a chance to react, she was already getting splashed by Callie Ann's swan dive into the ocean. Lena ran to the other side of the deck in time to see her best friend swimming rapidly ashore. With anyone else, you might be worried, but Callie Ann Connors had been captain of the state champion swim team for the last two years. The girl had some serious skills in the water and a lust for risk-taking Lena had so far only seen in boys.

Callie Ann pulled herself up onto the beach and waved to Lena. Her clothes drenched, her hair matted with seaweed, Callie Ann still managed to look like a swimsuit model. Good thing she lived just a few yards back from the water's edge, Lena thought, casting a worried eye along the shore line. God forbid those college boys jogging along the beach saw her, drenched, her T-shirt clinging....

Hold it. What was *that*?

As Callie Ann ran off home, Lena's head whipped around seaward, at the explosive crack of what ... sounded like ... a sonic boom — and that made no sense. Sure, inexperienced pilots got themselves twisted up flying over the ocean once in a while. But none of them, she was pretty sure, were going faster than the speed of sound.

As the sky started to darken for nightfall, the ear-snapping sound of a second sonic boom was preceded by a thin streak of orange light, heading straight into the ocean at a 45-degree angle.

"No way *that* was an airplane," Lena said to the sky.

And in the space of that tiny moment of reflection, she realized she had a problem on her hands. With Callie Ann gone, Lena was out on the boat alone. She should turn back but — gross — by now Dad and Rhea were probably making out on the sofa. Even if she hadn't wanted to spoil it for him, the thought of seeing two middle-aged people wrapped around each other? She'd rather eat sea snails for breakfast.

So what should she do? Considering the ruckus of the sonic boom and the piercing orange light that followed it, Lena was sure the Coast Guard would have been out there by now. But what was she thinking? The World Cup was on. Could be, the Coast Guard was distracted.

Could be, she was grasping at straws.

Lena had known the guys at the Coast Guard Marina for years, ever since Dad decided he'd rather run a tour boat off Felicity Bay every summer than teach summer school back in Skudderton. It was the one thing Mom had never let him do. Anyway, Captain Halpern wouldn't allow soccer to get in the way of policing the Bay. Even if this was the first year the American team could be taken seriously. But where was he?

Looking out over the water where the plane — if that's what it was — had gone down, Lena realized something was wrong with her eyesight. No matter how she turned her head, she couldn't focus on the exact spot on the horizon where she'd seen the orange flame hit the water. The closer she got, the faster her gaze would bounce off toward a different point on the horizon.

"Don't even think of hiding from me," she whispered. Summoning every ounce of concentration, she took her head in her hands and pointed it right at the spot in the ocean where....

Thirty minutes later, Lena awoke in the cruiser's cabin, lying next to the half refrigerator, an empty can of beer held tight in each hand.

Whoa. Not that she'd never had beer before — but never in such a totally uncool way. How would she explain the missing cans to Dad? More important, how could she explain them to herself? Clutching the arm of a small leather love seat, she pulled herself up to her feet.

"Oh my God, I actually drank these," she whispered. Yet as startled as she was, another surprise waited for her when she crawled back out to the deck. Not only was the *Shari Lynn* tied up at the marina, but there at her feet was a small, sealed envelope, the kind you got when you were invited to a wedding — or a funeral. Lena's hands shook as she picked up the pristine ivory-colored envelope and studied the perfectly inscribed letters, "Ms. Lena Gabrilowicz"

OK, what the ... jelly fish ... was this?

Still shaken by the events of the last few minutes, Lena's first impulse was to toss the envelope into the ocean. But there was Officer Gründlich walking past on the marina. Lena didn't have to guess what the officer's reaction would be to the sight of someone throwing junk into the ocean. The last thing she wanted was to get on Marta's bad side — especially considering the officer was Dad's old girlfriend.

Might as well open the mysterious envelope and let whoever was pranking her get it out of his system. Probably Gary Reynolds, come to think of it. Why couldn't he either ask her out or leave her alone? Yet, taking a second look, she realized the envelope had a totally "un-Gary" quality.

Funny how perfectly dry and fresh it stayed, no matter how long it hung out with Lena in the ocean-drenched air, no matter how roughed up it got by her grubby thumbs ... There.... What did it say? Wiping away a grain of sand at the corner of her eye, Lena unfolded the beautifully crafted ivory note paper and read a single sentence inscribed in fussy calligraphy:

No one will believe you.

A second later, the note paper and the envelope were just so much ivory-colored dust clinging to Lena's fleshy fingers. And though she clapped her hands together several times, it stayed put. Looking out across the bay, she found she now had no trouble focusing her eyes on any part of the ocean. "The spot," whatever it was, was gone. Tears rolled down her cheeks and she staggered a bit as she stalked over to the weather side of the boat for a better look.

Nothing: What kind of scary prank was this?

On the other hand, what kind of local prankster could create an illusion like that? OK, maybe a neighborhood kid could build a humongous kite, set it on fire and let it blow out over the ocean. But why go to the trouble? And that sound: Whether it was an experimental jet or a military bombing raid, Lena was sure nothing that loud ever popped out the end of a firecracker.

Heaving a deep sigh, she tried to steady herself against the railing of the *Shari Lynn*. But she had no sooner slowed down her breathing than she remembered the open beer cans from the half refrigerator.

Squeezing into the cabin, she was surprised to see the tiny galley swept as clean and neat as the day Dad bought the *Shari Lynn* four years ago. Come to think of it, Lena wasn't quite sure she'd ever seen it that clean. Not knowing what to expect, she tiptoed over to the half refrigerator and opened its fake, wood-patterned door. Snug up against the right wall on the top shelf was a full six pack of Rolling Rock, exactly as Dad had left it earlier that afternoon.

"Cool," said Lena, her face lighting up with an odd combination of mischief and relief that, for a moment, bathed her mind in the sweet glow of normality. But the effect didn't last. Lena Gabrilowicz, Junior at Skudderton High and fan of everything Louise Nevelson had ever sculpted, knew what she'd seen. And what she'd seen was definitely not just a lame prank.

CHAPTER THREE

By time of splashdown on the alien world, the transmog chamber had finished its gruesome business. Flat on his back, Ixdahan tried to assess the situation. In the plus column, the shaking, oozing and vomiting were over. In the minus column, he was now a member of a totally alien species.

"Better test my legs," he told himself.

Too bad it wasn't that simple. Unable to find his center of gravity in a gaseous atmosphere, he lunged forward too fast — and flung himself face down to the lander's hard metallic floor. Had he broken his new calcium phosphate-based endoskeleton?

Sensing no pain, he pulled his knees up under him and paused before pushing himself up to his feet. He let his eyes flutter shut as he tried to steady his breathing. So far, the alien body worked fine — overlooking, of course, its one major drawback.

"Disgusting," he mumbled.

His stomach lurched as he forced himself to touch his new forehead for the first time. The image of the human body posted on the Galactic Array was revolting enough. But this ... it was hard to imagine anything worse. His new head was dry, bulbous and topped with a soft outgrowth; the fingers he used to probe it were stubby, boney, clawed.

Hands? Head? Fingers? Words from an alien language bubbled up into his consciousness from the Array. Hands, he saw in a flash of implanted memory, were for grasping tools, climbing trees and pressing a soft pair of lips into his....

What?

How could any sentient species survive with such poor mental discipline? He hadn't experienced so much cognitive drift since age five.

As he flopped down on his bed, Ixdahan struggled to accept the implications: The Earth creatures' psychological development was stunted. They were pre-mentallic, like many of the species he'd dealt with on the Homeworld.

He shuddered, remembering the oily traders and craven merchants who had lined the game rooms and holodecks — and fed his addiction to expensive forms of entertainment.

Should have just killed me, he thought.

Trouble was, they hadn't; he'd just have to get used to this ... existence. But how? As a teenager on Snaldrialoor, he'd been in control of his mind. On Earth, crammed into a human body, he couldn't predict how its hormonal fluctuations and transitional neural pathways might muddy his thoughts.

Yet he could also sense some other influence, reshaping him, for now his memory of the Homeworld was fuzzy, the outlines, distorted ...

Enough. According to the terms of his exile, his robotic caretakers were programmed to help him adapt.

"Better get started," said Ixdahan aloud, and was shocked by the bizarre sounds bouncing off the lander's curved walls. Of course, as any Homeworld neurologist could have told him, his mind hadn't yet adjusted to perceiving sound waves through a gaseous atmosphere.

"DXN/GRG!" Ixdahan yelled in his slightly cracked voice.

The door to his cabin slid open to reveal one of two DXN-series robots, a likeness of a sentient Earth creature, about 42 cycles old — and absolutely hideous.

But that was nothing compared to the way it talked.

"Hi ya, Son," the DXN unit said in a broad accent. "Finally made it up, Sleepy Head? Your mom and I were gettin' kinda worried."

Ixdahan's human eyes bulged.

"Is this how you speak to your master?" he snapped.

Without a word, the DXN unit shook its head and plopped down on the plump, leatherette love seat to Ixdahan's left.

"That's my boy," it said, with a precisely calibrated human chuckle, "But I'm gonna have to ask you to keep your sense of humor on the back burner when your mom's around. She's been worried sick: Thought you might wake up dead."

"That's enough," said Ixdahan through clenched teeth. "Homeworld protocol dictates...."

"Now, you see, Son, I got to say I'm disappointed in you," said the robot. "Thought you would've figured out a few things by now," he added. "Like maybe protocol has changed — what with your exile and all?"

Before Ixdahan could answer, he felt a pair of bio-mechanical hands spin him around by the shoulders to face a full-length mirror on the opposite wall.

"There," said DXN/GRG, "get a good look at yourself. See any changes in protocol you'd like to talk about?"

Ixdahan's eyebrows arched.

"It's not my fault they made me look like a dork," he heard himself whine.

Dork? What had the Consortium done to his speech centers?

"Now, Son," said the DXN unit, "we'll have plenty of time to deal with what-you-call your 'Acculturation Issues' when we get set up in our new home. For now, try to appreciate how thorough the folks in Transmog were."

"Thorough?" asked Ixdahan.

"Exactly," said the robot with a wink. "Whatever you was before, forget about it. Right now? Today? You're human. And I," the DXN unit added, leaning in, "I'm your Daddy."

Turning back to the mirror, Ixdahan fought hard against his tears. He knew what the cool kids looked like and this was *definitely* not it.

"Not fair!" he said ... but ... but there it was again, a sure sign he was losing control of his mind.

"This mentallic interference is unacceptable!" he roared with his scratchy, uneven voice.

"Interference?" the DXN unit cut in. "Don't get ahead of yourself, Boy. The Transmog folks just wanted you to fit right in with your new home. You ought to be grateful."

"I get it," said Ixdahan drying his eyes with his palms. "I look like a dweeb for my own good."

Dweeb? It was like having two brains, only one of which worked properly.

"Don't take it so hard, Derek," said the robot. "Your mom can help you spruce up and look your best."

"She can *what?*" yelled Ixdahan. "No, don't answer that. Tell me who this 'Derek' is."

The robot eyed him, its jaw tensing.

"Did you read the file I posted on the ol' Array, Son?"

"Yes," whispered Ixdahan.

"Then you know. Your name is Derek Dixon," DXN/GRG continued. "You're 17 Earth years old and you live with your Daddy, George (that's me) and your Mom, Sarah, whom you might be tempted to call DXN/SRH. But I'd advise against it."

Ixdahan cringed as the robot clapped a humanoid arm around his shoulders and said, "Now, you want to reread that file? Hurry it up, though, I don't have forever."

"Don't take that tone with me!" said Ixdahan, as DXN/SRH appeared at the doorway.

"Hey now, Young Man," she chirped. "Is my big boy tired from his long trip? How about I make you a nice, hot lunch?"

"I demand an explanation!" Ixdahan/Derek said. "The Consortium has overstepped its authority...."

But DXN/SRH held up her hand for silence and Ixdahan's mouth went dry. Why was it impossible to speak?

"You settle yourself down and get dressed, Derek Dixon," said his robotic mom, fixing his eyes with a stern glare, "and then I'll get your lunch ready."

"Yes, Mom," said Ixdahan. And as he watched "Sarah Dixon" glide out of his quarters, he wondered how far the Consortium's mind control went.

"See?" said DXN/GRG, patting his cheek. "Things aren't so bad. Now, hurry up, get dressed and then I'll explain a few things. Watch your manners, and I might let you go exploring on your own."

The moment the robot glided out of his room, Ixdahan flung himself face down on his bed, screaming and pounding his pillow. But, strangely, even his fury didn't stop him from noticing how snuggly soft and clean the sheets felt against his naked body. Mom sure went to a lot of trouble to make things nice for him....

Wait. What was he thinking — *and why was he thinking it*?

The way he shut down when DXN/SRH raised her hand ... obviously the robots' cortical dampeners had taken over his mind. Breathing hard, Ixdahan Daherek, once a proud member of an ancient Snaldrialooran family, cried into his pillow like the high-strung Earth boy he had become.

That is, until the rumbling in his stomach and the delicious smell of beef stew coming from the galley made him jump out of bed, rummage through his closet and pull on some clothes. Sure, he realized, the robots were controlling his mood, even adjusting it on a moment-by-moment basis. But he didn't — *couldn't* — care. Right now? Today? It was lunchtime and he, Derek Dixon, was seriously hungry.

CHAPTER FOUR

Looking out over the bay from the boathouse, Lena forced herself to accept that summer was over. Objectively, it was obvious. Time passed, days ticked by and the flow of tourists came to a halt. But every year it took longer to sink in.

Now, alone in the ticket booth — as she watched greasy squares of wax paper tumble out of overstuffed garbage cans and flit aimlessly in the breeze off the ocean — she knew. Tomorrow afternoon, following Dad's last run with the tour boat, he'd hustle back to their rented cottage and start stuffing his duffel bags for the trip home.

Already, the *Shari Lynn*, Dad's creaky, 22-foot cat boat cruiser, was moored and stowed — the saddest reminder that the season had caught up to her again. And yet, as usual, the idea of settling back into Skudderton was also kind of a relief. For one thing, she could see Arkansas again, the black and white Tom cat they always left with a neighbor for the summer.

"And no sand in the sheets at night," she mumbled into the hand currently propping up her sunburned face. But leaving the shoreline took her farther away from her fading memories of Mom — who had looked so happy and so in love with Dad and every little shell on the beach.

Did Mom "know," or was that a cliché from the movies? Lena knew where she stood. So far, nothing in real life could convince her that people were guided by visions, omens or signs. Stuff happened and you had to deal with it, like Mom dying of a heart attack, or Silvano moving away to Milan.

Silvano was the perfect example. His dad had taken a job with an Italian film production company just when Lena and Silvano were starting to feel close. Seemed like no matter what she wanted in life, Reality always interfered.

Left on her own in the tiny ticket booth, Lena had way too much time to make herself miserable. Leaving Harmony Beach meant letting go of Mom. Going back to Skudderton meant obsessing over Silvano Costa, the one boy on Earth who could see past her lack of "Callie Ann-ness."

In a rational world, no guy would find Lena Gabrilowicz unattractive. She smiled easily, remembered your birthday and was there for you when you were having a homework meltdown. Get her started about the ocean and she'd get all poetic — then crack you up with that story about her dad tripping over the ropes and landing face down in a bucket of fresh sea bass.

But high school is probably the most irrational place on the face of the planet and Lena's lack of Callie Ann-ness was the only thing most boys noticed. Except, that is, for sweet, romantic Silvano....

"One for the tour," said a slightly cracked voice to the ticket booth window.

Lena whipped her head around to see a nervous, yet nice-looking guy staring up at her.

"It's the last tour of the day, and it doesn't start until three forty-five," she said, as officially as she could with her head still full of Silvano. "You OK with that?"

"Whatever," said the boy, who Lena figured was probably her own age. But as he dug a few bills out of a brand new pair of jeans, he looked as clumsy as a six-year-old.

"Is there anything to do around here until then?"

Lena cocked her head to one side and counted to 10 while making his change.

"A lot of people like to sunbathe or go for a swim," she said, "but I don't think you're dressed for it."

The boy shrugged and stared off at the ocean.

"First time at the beach," he said, "didn't know what to expect. Anyway, don't I need pressurized oxygen tanks?"

Lena bit her lip.

"That's only if you want to go scuba diving," she said. "You'd have to go.... Well, look," she said, as her curiosity got the better of her, "I just sold you the last ticket for the three forty-five, so I might as well close up. Why don't I show you around myself?"

"Thanks," said the boy, "but I can't pay you. I gave you all the money I have."

Right, thought Lena. You handed me a hundred dollars for a $14.75 boat tour.

"No charge," she said, as she rushed to open the register, chuck the till in the mini-vault, flick off the lights, slip out of the booth and lock the door behind her. Dad would get steamed if he saw her leave without zeroing out the register, but she figured she'd handle that while he was out on the tour boat.

"Here's your change," she said, stuffing a wad of bills and a few coins into the boy's dress shirt pocket which, by the way, was made of English linen. "What's your name? Mine's Lena."

"Derek," said the boy with a wince, "Derek Dixon."

"Welcome to Harmony Beach," said Lena softly. Not that it made any sense, but this guy was kind of cute. You'd think he were proud of how clueless he was.

And that, Lena realized, made him a rare find. Outside of Silvano, the only boys who showed an ounce of self-reflection were the ones on movie screens. Of course, these days, Silvano was also available only onscreen; if she wanted to be with him, it had to be on Facebook, AIM or Skype.

Unlike Silvano, this kid acted like he was half computer. She no sooner pointed out the sea crabs washing up on the sand than he rattled off facts about their Paleozoic ancestors. At least, she *thought* that's what he said. Funny thing was, even though Derek didn't have a foreign accent, it sounded like he'd learned English only yesterday.

"Do you ... do you live here year round?" asked Derek.

"I wish," said Lena, sizing him up sneakily. With that thick, wavy hair, he was borderline handsome — as long as she didn't focus on that baby-face skin and the wobbly way he lurched around on the sand.

Looking out at the water again — no sense in tipping her hand — she saw Callie Ann playing in the tide and waved at her without thinking.

"So, where *do* you live?" asked the boy, pausing to wipe the sand off his perfectly creased jeans. At the shoreline, Callie Ann was running towards them, her one-piece swimsuit clinging to her torso like a second skin.

"Up in Skudderton," said Lena, cursing herself as Callie Ann came bouncing up to greet her.

"Hi Lena Lovely," said Callie Ann, as moodily sweet as she was moodily sour the night before. "Who's your friend?"

"I'm Derek," said the boy, holding out his hand. "Do you live in Skudderton, too?"

Glancing at him sideways, Lena felt a knot forming in her stomach. How come this gawky, shy kid was now so self-confident?

From then on, she knew it was hopeless. The Callie Ann Effect had taken hold again.

Shaking the boy's hand, Lena's best friend tossed her long blond hair, sending flecks of refracted afternoon sun bouncing this way and that in the breeze. The boy, Lena noticed, hadn't offered to shake hands with her when they met.

"Good thing," she mumbled, looking down at her swollen fingers and palms. They were covered with stiff, ivory-colored lumps, the remains of the mysterious envelope she'd picked up on the *Shari Lynn*.

In the right light, the lumps looked like some kind of mutated fungus. Peeling them off was impossible — and rubbing her hands together made them burn something fierce. Thinking back to last night's sighting, Lena wondered what else that fiery blaze might have left behind.

Wait. Was she ... losing her balance? Bent double in the hot sand, she thought she was going to pass out....

And yet, the next second, she heard herself giggling hard at ... at what? Must have been some raunchy compliment Callie Ann had shouted to the lifeguard who was now jogging past.

"She's always pulling stuff like this," said Lena to the sand between her toes. Squinting in the bright sun, Lena shook her head at the sight of Callie Ann sprinting to catch up with the muscular jogger. But what if the guy took her seriously? And what would Blain Northop say? Not that she cared. "Blade," as they called him at school, was the worst kind of....

"You OK?" asked strange little Derek, who was emptying the sand from his hand-crafted Italian loafers.

"Sure," said Lena, "must be the sun. Come on," she added, patting the boy's back a little too hard. "It's almost time for the tour."

CHAPTER FIVE

Late that night in the Snaldrialooran lander, the DXN units were busy preparing for a quantum transfer to their permanent home base on Earth. Meanwhile, the youngest intergalactic criminal on record was stuck on his bed, plowing through hundreds of acculturation modules.

Ixdahan's heart sank as he stared at the slim tablet computer that DXN/GRG had shoved into his hands. Aided by the cortical dampeners implanted by the transmog process, his metadigital wardens now kept him tightly controlled.

"Can't let them ... erase me," he whispered. Tossing the tablet down on his bed, he tapped into the Galactic Array and monitored the data flow from the two robots. Lucky for him, they were totally preoccupied with their q-transfer calculations.

His head swirling, Ixdahan tugged at the neuro-suppressor implanted under the skin of his left forearm. By creating barely detectable electromagnetic interference patterns, it partially curtailed his native telepathic abilities. Though he could still connect to the Array and receive passive mentallic impressions from Earth people, he could only actively engage another mind in cases of life-threatening danger.

Not that his current situation seemed like anything less. Imagine attempting to master an alien language and culture with silicon chips encased in polymers, glass and aluminum!

Of course, the only thing in real danger was his self-esteem, and that was in rough shape— his one shred of dignity being a single m-mail posted on the Array. It was a note from cousin Jalgren Altrollinhar, a professor at Lohaar University, and the only member of House Daherek to keep up with Ixdahan after his parents split up.

"Nice work," the note read. "One of my colleagues is a legal consultant for the Consortium. Maybe she can get your sentence commuted to time served. Until then, you'll have to make do with only four tentacles."

"Five," muttered Ixdahan, recalling the many sleepless nights he'd suffered since emerging from the transmog chamber.

It would have felt good to answer Jalgren, but direct communication with the Homeworld was banned. Besides, he needed to focus on absorbing what he could of human history, culture and ethics.

But as the lessons droned on, Ixdahan's mind wandered back to yesterday's field mission along the shoreline. Trouble was, his memory was sketchy ... yes, there it was again ... the distinct sensation that entire areas of his consciousness were misfiring.

Finally, using every mental trick he knew, Ixdahan managed to revisit his tour of the beach with the female ... with Lena. Yes, that was it: He'd met her only minutes after q-transferring to an abandoned umbrella stand about 100 meters from the shore.

At first, she'd seemed as hideous as his own reflection in the mirror. In time, he discovered her voice had a lilting quality missing from the modulated tones generated by DXN/SRH's precision-crafted acoustical system. Besides, despite the limitations of her species, Lena's observations revealed her to be a sentient creature like himself, curious about the texture of the universe and the meaning of life.

But nothing had prepared him for the sensations he felt when she laughed. Her laughter initiated a sequence of pleasurable sensations he had first encountered at the very end of the transmog process. What did that mean? And why had the sensations intensified when Lena introduced him to Callie Ann, her "BFF"? He'd been shaken down to his bone marrow at the sight of the mid-afternoon sun shining directly through her sandy blond hair.

Stranger still, Lena had become sullen and quiet, even when Callie Ann had run off. Why was that?

"Time to go, Derry Boy," said George Dixon's sunny voice behind him. Ixdahan's blood ran cold.

"DXN/GRG!," he shouted. "I gave you a direct order not to address me in that fashion." Within a nano-second, he was thrashing about on the floor of the lander — as pulsing waves of pain scorched every nerve-ending in his newly transmogged body.

George tucked a late-model *djalcrohloor* back into his jacket pocket.

"And I," he said, "instructed you not to address me by my serial number."

The pain subsided. Ixdahan picked his shaky, pee-soaked body off the floor and hung his head.

"Sorry Dad," he said. "It won't happen again."

"That's my boy," said George, patting him on the shoulder. "Go on now, get changed. I'm pretty darn sure you don't want that mess you made getting merged into your legs for good."

Yes, thought Ixdahan, grabbing the towel and the change of clothes Sarah held out to him. The Consortium had spared itself the expense of a state-of-the-art transfer module. This piece of junk probably came from an agricultural colony on Ghalidreanthalis 2. He had to be completely dry so as not to confuse the scanners.

Yet 10 minutes later, fully recovered, Ixdahan was staring out at a weed-free lawn through the bay window of his new home. For now, he felt more comfortable in his alien skin. If only he could override the cortical dampeners and regain control of his mind. Bad enough to be stuck in a human body. Did he also have to act like a clumsy child?

Nodding, Ixdahan realized his exile was only a means to an end. Humiliation was his real punishment — to be stripped of the very mental abilities that had enabled him to commit his crime.

All the same, he did have one tiny victory. Snaldrialooran relocation protocols, as it turned out, restricted the robots to a narrow range of triangulations. The location had to be far from any industrial base, military installation or other technology center that might detect their extra-terrestrial origins. And among the acceptable options was the quiet dwelling cadre called "Skudderton," where the insightful Lena and spectacular Callie Ann had their primary residences.

Moving in fast, he invoked *khaldahrn drolghar* and the matter was settled. The robots' programming demanded unquestioned compliance. Yet, what could he expect from the "high school" they insisted he attend to maintain appearances?

"Maybe get a date with Callie Ann," his mind raced.

And in that moment, he was distracted long enough for the DXN units to act. Exerting pressure on his sub-cortical memory centers, they firmly implanted his new identity. As long as he was under their direct control, the former heir to L'han Singha Province would see himself as "Derek Dixon."

Left to their own logic circuits, the two late-model AIs would have erased his mind and installed implanted memories of a childhood on Earth. Lucky for Ixdahan, memory-substitution was reserved for the gravest interstellar crimes. Memory-wipe a juvenile offender with a technology not yet fully understood? Unthinkable.

Instead, the Interstellar Consortium opted for a more limited reorganization of the boy's neural pathways: "Prisoner Daherek, Case Log H+ZQ/^KL@7" would remember only those aspects of his former life that were essential to maintaining his sanity and ensuring his survival.

CHAPTER SIX

Out at Skudderton-Thornberry Mall, down the cavernous aisles of the 'Senshals Super Store, Lena squeezed her eyes shut and stopped her cart. Between the harsh florescent lighting and the huge day-glo signage, she was on her way to a giant tension headache. Maybe she shouldn't have come on her own.

Used to be, Lena did her back-to-school shopping with Mom. After Mom ... after she ... Dad tagged along for moral support and drove the sales clerks crazy — asking about price, value, durability. Still, with her head throbbing, Lena felt an urge to swing home and drag Dad out to the mall for company.

"Deal with it," she muttered.

This was 'Senshals, not a horror movie — the kind Silvano used to make her watch with him. What was up with that? Two hours of decaying mummies, murderous puppets or gloopy, sloppy, blood-sucking monsters? And the screaming....

Soon, memories of snuggling up against Silvano in front of Dad's flatscreen had eased Lena out of meltdown mode. Taking a deep breath, she let go of the cart handle — why did her fingers ache so much? — and sat down on the navy blue industrial carpet.

Funny how fast her life was changing, with Silvano off in Italy and Dad acting so weird. This morning, instead of taking Lena to the mall, Dad had handed her a wad of bills and the keys to the Touareg and told her to be home for dinner. Lena wanted to believe this meant he trusted her more, now that she was a Junior.

But, deep down, she knew it was because of Rhea. Dad had invited his new Harmony Beach girlfriend to hang out in Skudderton for the last week of August. Come to think of it, "home for dinner" might be a coded message. Dad, Lena realized, loved her too much to *ask* her to stay away. But that wouldn't stop him from hoping she'd figure things out on her own.

"Well, guess what, Dad?" Lena muttered, her head resting against a package of mailing labels. "I'm so totally on to you."

Besides, what was the problem? She handled tons of chores on her own now. These days, almost anything outside of teaching and boating was more than Dad could deal with. Good thing he'd put the utility bills on direct deposit; she didn't even want to be anywhere near him if the electricity got shut off.

The thought of Dad in a panic made Lena giggle a little too loud. That earned her a quizzical stare from the beautiful woman down the aisle. But who did she remind Lena of?

"Mom, you think I need these optical discs?" said a scratchy voice from around the corner.

"Not sure, Derek Dear," said DXN/SRH with a wink at Lena, "why don't you ask this nice young lady what she thinks?"

Rushing to her feet, Lena almost collided with the gawky boy she'd met at Harmony Beach last week.

"Wow, sorry," said Derek. "Hey, it's you, isn't it — Lena?"

Great. Why was she wearing her baggiest pants ever?

"How's ... how's your friend, Callie Ann?" asked Derek, his eyes wide.

"Derry?" asked Sarah Dixon, as a flurry of algorithms in her vocal processors added a note of impatience to her voice.

"Mom, this is Lena," said Derek, his voice trembling.

Lena thought nothing of reaching over to shake hands with Derek's mom — but the moment their fingers touched, the robot's face became blank, lifeless.

"You OK ... Mom?" asked Derek.

"I'm fine, Dear," said DXN/SRH in a monotone. Derek looked worried, but Lena figured she must have heartburn or whatever. Adults were such a mess!

"I'll go ask that nice man at the counter about those darn discs," Sarah Dixon piped up. Gazing after her, Lena marveled at her perfect posture and gliding walk.

"Sorry," said Derek, looking after her, "my mom...."

"It's OK," said Lena, "all parents are weird."

But if Lena expected a high-five or an I-hear-that from Derek, it wasn't happening. His idea of small talk was fidgeting with his sneakers.

"Callie Ann's fine, by the way," said Lena, anxious to break the silence. "But she always waits until the last minute to get ready for school."

"Isn't that kind of ... inefficient?" asked Derek.

"Inefficient?" laughed Lena. "Not when your shopping strategy is to borrow stuff from your friends."

"So, you don't ... like ... Callie Ann anymore?" asked Derek.

"No ... I mean, yes," said Lena, "but everybody has flaws."

"Yeah, I know. Where I come from...." Derek started.

"Where is that, anyway?" asked Lena. This she had to hear.

"Lansing," said Derek at last, as if he were reading it off an index card. "Lansing, Michigan. You've heard of it?"

"Yeah, I've heard of Planet Earth, too," Lena snorted. "Sorry," she added, "I'm in a weird mood. I wasn't expecting to run into anyone today. That's why I look like a wreck."

Derek's eyes opened wide.

"Can I ask you something?" he whispered, "Am I dressed OK?"

"You look fine," said Lena, almost believing her own lie. After all, if this had been the stage of a teen talent show, he would have fit right in. Smiling, Lena chose a pen from the "TRY ME" bin at the end of the aisle, grabbed Derek's hand and scribbled on his palm.

"If you're choked up about your look, check out that site," she said. "Don't worry, it's for guys, too."

Derek hesitated, staring at his hand.

"Could we view it together," he said, "at your house?"

"Your mom coming?" asked Lena.

"Looks like it's a 'no' on these optical discs," said Sarah Dixon, gliding back into the aisle.

"Mom," said Derek, "can you drop me off at Lena's now?"

"Un-be-lievable," thought Lena, considering Derek probably only wanted new clothes to impress Callie Ann.

"Can't now," said Lena. "I just started shopping."

"Right," said Derek, looking crushed.

Maybe there was hope for a guy who knew when he was being a dork, Lena realized. Better cut him a break....

"Catch up with you at school next week and we'll figure something out, OK?" said Lena.

"Next week," said Derek, as Lena backed her cart out of the aisle and headed for the opposite end of the store as fast as possible — before Derek could ask for her cell number.

An hour later, Lena rolled into her driveway and shut off the engine. Better give Dad a couple minutes. But while the driveway was shaded by the big Colorado blue spruce in the front lawn, the late August heat took only a few minutes to scorch up the car. Time to go in. After a quick, embarrassed hello at the doorway, Lena ran upstairs and shut herself up in her room.

"It's going to be different this year, I swear," she whispered, "but I have to get my act together."

In Art class last spring, she'd gotten a feel for metalwork sculpture, and now she wanted make it into a top Art School. For that, she needed a kick-ass portfolio, a better average — and she'd have to *focus*. Good luck with that. When she wasn't doodling sculpture designs, her mind would fill up with the thought of millions of species down under sea level — swimming, crawling, fighting for survival....

"Stop it!" she said, clapping her hands. How come every time she made up her mind what she wanted to do with her life, the ocean would call to her with its soft, splashy voice?

Looking out her window at the sun rolling down over Gary Reynolds' house, Lena realized she didn't have to decide right away. She'd sign up for A.P. Bio *and* Metal Shop and see which way her sails were pointed in January.

"And now can I please get to work?" she said to the framed photo of Silvano that stared out at her from her desk. Before long, she was in a good rhythm: folders on the left, pens and pencils on the right....

Except, what was up with her hands?

They'd been getting stiffer all the way home from the mall. Now, by the light of her desk lamp, it looked like that envelope she'd found on the *Shari Lynn* had burrowed under her skin. But how was that possible unless the envelope wasn't really....

Half an hour later, she woke up, sprawled out on her bed. Was she really so tired? But OK, maybe she could make progress before she had to cook dinner. That is, if she could find the....

"So that's where I put the scissors!" she blurted out. Giggling, she couldn't help noticing how well her words would fit that old Dark Matter song:

So....
That's where I put the scissors:
Right up inside my heartache,
Piercing the burning agony of doom!

Soon she was dancing and cleaning and dancing and cleaning....

"Lena, dinner," Dad's voice echoed up the stairwell.

That was a switch. Usually, meals were Lena's department. Dad's idea of cooking was buying a barbecued chicken and boiling up some string beans. What a shock to see the table laid out the way it used to be, right down to the old-fashioned glass mold, now emerald green with lime Jell-O. After running into strange little Derek and his Mom, chowing down with Dad and Rhea was a big relief. Best of all, Rhea didn't go all Parental on her.

"Looking forward to school?" Rhea asked with a wink during dessert. OK, that was a standard adult question, but the nice part was, Rhea seemed to understand that. So when dinner was over and Dad was busy shoving dishes into the dishwasher, Lena thought nothing of it when Rhea offered to read her palm.

"I used to do this to earn a little extra money right out of college," said Rhea, her deep-set brown eyes flashing with laughter. "So don't take it too seriously."

That sounded like fun — if only the house didn't have to feel so hot, even with the AC on high. Maybe sitting quietly with Rhea would help her cool off. So, expecting to hear about her life line, Lena held out her palm — and heard Rhea shriek.

"Todd! We have to get Lena to the hospital!"

The room began to spin. Worse, the harder Lena tried to explain what had happened, the more confused she got.

"There wasn't an airplane?" she yelled, jumping to her feet, "There was! I saw it, burning up in the sky. I saw it...."

Lena trembled as her senses splintered like light through a kaleidoscope. She felt herself fall to the floor, then felt her Dad scoop her up; she heard the sound of the car starting, and a whole lot of anxious talk as the Touareg bounced around on the highway out to Skudderton General. By the time the ER orderlies had lifted her onto a gurney, Lena was out cold.

CHAPTER SEVEN

For an extra-terrestrial who was still getting used to the concept of feet, Derek's first day of high school was fairly uneventful. Anyone else would have called it a nightmare.

Nothing in the DXN-units' metadigital acculturation modules had prepared him for *this*: The preening, the pranking, the shouting, the bizarre intimidation rituals — and the tidal wave of sexual tension tumbling out of 1,200 voracious teenage minds.

In fact, the only thing protecting Derek from an emotional meltdown was his passive mentallic link to the Galactic Array:

> *Objective 1:*
> *Approach Welcome Desk.*
> *Obtain Home Room, Class and*
> *Section Assignments from Student*
> *Advisory Representative....*

Yet the Array did have a few limitations. Despite its galaxy-spanning capacity, it was unable to predict what Gary Reynolds would do the second Derek walked away from the Welcome Desk. The explanation was simple: The critical variable involved was the *only* variable in the known universe the Galactic Array was incapable of processing: Abject Stupidity.

That Gary would chuck his left sneaker into the hallway at just the right moment to send Derek sprawling into the open door of the girl's bathroom was inconceivable. Or so it would have been to the inter-species panel of programming consultants who had managed the Array for countless generations.

Any Earth kid could have seen it coming all the way from the moons of Jupiter.

Now, if Derek were confused about Gary's motives, the reaction he got from the girl who was already halfway through the bathroom door was cause for serious bewilderment.

"Gross, you little creep," snarled Callie Ann, "were you crawling in to spy on me?"

"Can't breathe...." said Derek who, despite being shocked and winded, had the good sense not to look up at that moment. "Somebody ... tripped ... me," he added, gasping.

"You fell real good, too," said Gary Reynolds over a chorus of giggles and coughing horse laughs from his doofus fan base.

Still too frightened to move, Derek tried to steady himself by reciting a Snaldrialooran hymn under his breath. But the poem's reverent pleas to the spiritual overlords of the Homeworld felt out of place and, besides, his human voice box couldn't even pronounce most of the words.

Shaking her head, Callie Ann stepped over Derek's crumpled body, clomped straight up to Gary Reynolds in her sleek leather boots and slapped him hard across the mouth.

"What the freak is the matter with you?" she yelled. "Can't you see this kid is a total spaz?"

Gary opened his sore mouth to say something stupid, but he never got the chance. The class buzzer sounded for Home Room and everybody scattered — except Derek and Callie Ann.

"Get up," said Callie Ann to Derek, whose breathing was settling down. "You've got class."

"Think I broke a rib," said Derek.

"One way to find out," said Callie Ann. Crouching down beside him, she dug her fingers into his sides, tickling him without mercy. Derek shivered, feeling sensations no member of House Daherek had ever known before.

"Stop it!" he shrieked, and, to get away from her, he stood up faster than he thought possible.

"See?" said Callie Ann. "What's broken? C'mon, let's get you to class."

"Don't you also ... have class?" said Derek, longing for the liquid-methane oceans of Snaldrialoor.

"What? Home Room?" asked Callie Ann, rummaging through her backpack. "Forget it. I usually get the announcements and forms and stuff from Lena. You seen her today, by the way?"

"No," said Derek, his mind overheating at the sight of Callie Ann's over-sized jeans jacket falling off her right shoulder. "Maybe I'll skip, too."

"No way," said Callie Ann, pulling a stick of cinnamon gum from her backpack. "You're the new kid. Everybody's looking out for you today. Kind of nice, really."

And though Derek could point to one or two aspects of the current situation that weren't so nice, he decided not to complain. Far better to lose himself in Callie Ann's jade green eyes — not that she let him.

"I'll take you there myself," she said, pursing her lips. "Though I should probably take you to the nurse," she added, before hustling off down the hallway ahead of him.

Perplexed, Derek pulled himself together, tucked his shirt back in and hurried after her, wondering what the school nurse would make of his transmogged physiognomy.

"So where do you think Lena is?" asked Callie Ann as Derek struggled to catch up to her.

"I don't ... don't know," said Derek, breathing hard. "But when I saw her at the mall, her hands did seem to have acquired a parasitical fungus. Are they common on this ... in this area?"

"What the freak are you talking about?" asked Callie Ann, as they reached Home Room. "Oh crap," she said, swatting Derek's forearm. "Mrs. Halloway saw me. Now I have to go in."

"You kids want to take your seats?" said their teacher, smoothing out the wrinkles in her sky-blue pants suit. "First day's always crazy, I know. But we've got to get started, OK?"

Heads down, Derek and Callie Ann shuffled over to the two remaining seats.

"Nice going, ass-face," whispered Gary Reynolds' voice directly behind Derek. "Wait 'til Blade finds out you've been hittin' on his girl."

"Kind of looks like the only one getting hit on was you," sniped Callie Ann under her breath.

"Now," said the bright-eyed Mrs. Halloway, "we have a new student to welcome this year."

"New ass-face," muttered Gary Reynolds into his notebook.

For the rest of the period, Derek used every mental resource at his command to make sense of the situation. Though he could grasp the literal meaning of everything Mrs. Halloway said, much of it was seriously confusing. Trouble was, he was forced to wait until the Galactic Array provided an explanation.

As his DXN units had pointed out several times, asking Earth people questions about the everyday things they took for granted would immediately identify him as an outsider. The more basic the question, the greater the risk. Even the unstoppably positive Mrs. Halloway would have a hard time coping with the questions Derek wanted to ask about *everything*.

"Now guys," his teacher was saying, "if I've learned one thing in life, it's this: If you have a question, don't beat around the bush. Just ask. No one's going to shoot you."

Case in point: the idiomatic expression "Beat Around the Bush." What did landscape maintenance have to do with acquiring vital information? And why had this cryptic phrase made Gary Reynolds nearly choke on his own laughter?

It wasn't fair! Hadn't Derek already waded through stacks of acculturation modules? But no use whining about it, he scolded himself. If he was going to survive, he'd have to work things out on his own. Especially now that the one person who seemed to understand him was missing.

What had happened to Lena? She'd looked healthy a few days ago at the brightly-colored purchasing center — except for that odd fungal growth on her hands. The sight of it had reminded him of ... no, couldn't be ... not a slide from that boring exobiology class he'd taken at Gahaldoronek Prep last semester. A species from his galaxy turning up way out here?

And yet, he realized, as he copied the lunch schedule Mrs. Halloway was scribbling on the blackboard, he was a member of a species from that same galaxy. Well, it was probably nothing. Who knew what tricks the brutal transmog process had played on his memory? Before he could consider the answer, the thought of distant galaxies went tumbling out of his head as Mrs. Halloway turned her puffy torso his way.

"So, Derek," she said, pivoting on the heels of her sky-blue pumps, "we have a few minutes left. Why don't you tell us about who you are and where you're from?"

CHAPTER EIGHT

Fluttering back to consciousness, Lena stared at the layers of off-white gauze wrapped around her hands.

"What? How?" the splintered layers of her mind cried out. But soon the wave of questions crashing against her heart died down — replaced by a soothing ripple of calm.

The thing, whatever it was, was gone. Against a background of silent serenity, images from the past two weeks drifted through her memory, aligning themselves once again with the comforting, familiar reality of her life. Trouble was, it was the same reality in which she'd never see Mom again.

Lena sat up in bed — and looked for a way to keep her mind off ... that thought. As she glanced around her room, her eyes lit first on the oppressively cheerful color scheme of the Skudderton General Children's Ward.

"Must be nice to be so happy," she muttered, making a special point of ignoring the striped orange curtain drawn around her roommate's bed. Instead, she let her eyes settle on the get-well cards lined up on her side table.

How long had she been here? There must be six, no seven cards, including one from Aunt Kathy with a wide angle view of Lake Vancouver. And there, next to Dad's, was a card from strange little Derek, whose handwriting looked like it hadn't changed since Third Grade. But what had he written?

> *... hopefully the triazole treatments*
> *you receive will prevent the fungal*
> *growth from spreading through your*
> *lymphatic system and obviate radiation*
> *therapy, a potentially hazardous*
> *medical option....*

Reading the card over again, Lena couldn't decide if the bit about her treatment was any weirder than the P.S.

"I think Callie Ann likes me," he'd written under his babyish signature, which, Lena noticed, had taken him two tries to get right. Sure, everybody made mistakes, but what kind of dyslexia would make Derek start writing his name with the letters "Ix?"

"You're awake!" Dad's voice cut through her thoughts. Looking up from Derek's card, Lena's face broke out in a teary grin. As Dad's chapped lips touched her forehead, she wanted to reach up and throw her arms around his neck. But between the awkwardness of the gauze and the way her I.V. tube happened to be coiled around her bed rail, she barely missed slapping him in the face.

Not that she cared. No matter how many times Dad had driven her crazy in the last four years, his curly, salt and pepper hair and stubbly beard were the best thing for her mood.

"You look terrible, Daddy," Lena said, smiling.

"Sounds like the medicine's working," said Dad.

"What's the matter?" said Lena. "I'm fine." But the look in Dad's tired brown eyes seemed to disagree.

"Been a rough week," said Dad, dropping down into the visitor's chair by her bed. "The doctor said...."

His voice trailed off and he looked away. Her questions, Lena realized, would have to wait.

To give Dad his space, she picked up the card from Callie Ann that stood on her night table. "Love what you've done with your hands," the card read. In spite of herself, a smile spread itself over Lena's face. Just what you'd expect from your best friend, she thought.

"You're leaving today," said Dad, turning his head back to face Lena. "How's that?"

"Can't wait," she replied, still staring at Callie Ann's card, emblazoned with an impossibly muscular life guard on the front. "Hey Dad, when we get home, can you make sure Rhea's not there? I'm kind of embarrassed...."

Dad's jagged snores ripped right through the air around her. Looking up, she saw him asleep in the maroon vinyl hospital chair, relief relaxing his torso into a heap of muscle and bone. Too bad his snoring woke Lena's roommate, triggering a torrent of shrieks and gurgling sobs.

"What?" barked Dad, his body lurching forward.

"You woke up the baby," said Lena, smiling at his goofy expression.

"You had a baby?" he yawned, as his eyes snapped wide open.

Though she wanted to reassure him, Lena saw there was no point. Dad had dropped off to sleep again. And by the time a worried nurse charged in to check on Lena's infant roommate, Dad's snores were already filling the room again.

"He's been here round the clock for a week," said the nurse in a whisper as she pulled back the bright orange curtain around the baby's bed.

"Was it really that bad?" asked Lena, her stomach clenching.

"Better talk to the doctor," said the nurse, sliding the curtain shut around her and her patient.

"Guess so," said Lena, reaching for the one last card on her night stand, featuring a bright, colorful box kite soaring high in the air. But no sooner had she opened it than she flung it as far from her as was aerodynamically possible. Inside, she'd found a one-line message:

No one will believe you.

CHAPTER NINE

Down the hallways of Skudderton High, gossip zoomed into the fast lane, bouncing out of excitable mouths into eager ears. Fueled with the right mixture of titillation and intrigue, a juicy piece of gossip never missed its mark — raising eyebrows, tightening smiles and fluttering hearts.

For Derek, heading toward the lockers, the rush of excited chatter almost knocked him off his Nikes. On Snaldrialoor, ignoring gossip was much easier. Over time, you constructed a precisely tuned set of mental filters, ensuring only a fraction of the WorldThought reached your mind.

But here, among the humans, emotions were out in the open!

As he reached his locker in the five minutes between Math and English, the combined force of what he heard in his ears and sensed telepathically was overwhelming. Focusing his thoughts, he sorted his impressions into manageable layers.

One layer — the speedway of sexual longing Derek sensed in every student's mind — he confined in a Class 3 *thralchiadreal* field. Unfiltered, the force of so much erotic fantasy would have left him writhing in ecstasy on the tiled floor — not exactly what Principal Cosentino had in mind.

Shutting his eyes tight, Derek struggled to control his desires, strengthening the *thralchiadreal* field until it was fully established. Lucky for him, assigning Anxiety, Guilt, Violence and Aspiration to fields of their own would be much easier.

His head clearing, Derek narrowed his focus to concentrate on the two bits of gossip that got the most play. First, word was out that Lena Gabrilowicz was back from the hospital. Glad she was safe, news of her "recovery" still made Derek uneasy.

If the fungoid growth on her hands had originated offworld, the situation was more serious than her doctors realized. At most, they'd merely *suppressed* the alien fungus. What if it returned, subtler, deadlier?

Derek tried to put his fears in perspective by rearranging the books and papers in his locker. Better not to jump to conclusions, he decided. He had no clinical evidence that the fungus was extra-terrestrial.

What mattered most was that Lena, the one Earth creature he felt close to, was coming back into his life. That she was also the only one who could help him get closer to Callie Ann was secondary, he told himself, lying through his transmogged teeth. He hadn't stopped thinking about Callie Ann since he'd seen her hair blowing in the wind at Harmony Beach....

Better change the subject. What about the other bit of gossip that kept bubbling up: "mutant mailboxes"? Whatever they were, dozens of them had appeared overnight — from the bus terminal in South Skudderton, to the wide, upscale boulevards of Hunter's Wend.

Mysterious as the story was to the humans, Derek found it more puzzling still, since he found no reference to the mailboxes on the Galactic Array. Even generic search terms like "rounded blue storage vessel," returned zero results. What did that mean?

Some reference to these objects should have shown up — at least under the heading "Current Delusional Pathologies." OK, this was definitely one news item that would have made the list. The sudden appearance of mailboxes which no one could account for? Piles of undelivered mail turning up beside them, covered with thick, membranal slime? Incredible. Yet, it was even harder to believe that a story so widespread wasn't based in fact.

"You gonna just stand there, Kid?" demanded a voice six inches above his head. Looking up, Derek stared straight into a pair of brown eyes flickering behind thick, horn-rimmed glasses.

"Sorry," said Derek miserably. "Let me just...."

"Come ON!" insisted the mouth below the glasses, "I'm not gonna be late for AP Calc 'cause you're blocking my locker."

The hallway reverberated with the sound of a muscular arm slamming Derek's locker shut.

"Name's Vance," said the tall boy connected to the arm, the mouth and the glasses, as he spun through his locker combination with his thumb. "You always so spacey?" he asked.

"Yeah," said Derek hanging his head. "I am kind of spacey."

"So ... what ... you got antennas or something?" asked Vance with a grin.

"Tentacles," said Derek. Irony, he decided, was a lot easier to tolerate than a fist in the face.

"Hey, I like you, Man," said Vance, laughter crackling through his dark eyes — until he bounded away without looking back. "Tentacles!" he roared as he disappeared around the corner.

Shaking his head, Derek stowed his Math book and yanked out the fat paperback anthology Ms. Danielpoor insisted they bring to English each time. Imagine: Books!

Now, for the first time, Derek was grateful for the direct-to-cortex data transfers he'd received, ever since he was old enough to operate a metadigital tablet. Not that he'd ever put much of his education to use — but learning from books? Barbaric.

Yet the texture of the paper, the exotic perfume of the ink, the crinkle of the spine was alluring and that could only mean one thing: the Transmog Team had misaligned his senses.

"No way an assortment of cellulose fibers and organic pigments should be so seductive," he muttered, as he stepped into English class. Scurrying to the back, his eyes lit up at the sight of Lena, waving at him slyly with one bandaged hand. Funny how much prettier she looked when Callie Ann wasn't around.

"Heard about the mailboxes?" he asked, believing he'd finally grasped the breezy rhythms of casual human conversation.

"I'm fine now, thanks for asking," said Lena, reaching down to grab her pen from the floor. Derek cringed to see how she struggled to grasp it — with only the tips of her fingers poking out of the gauzy wrap covering her hands.

Staring at Lena, angry at himself for being so immature, Derek didn't notice his teacher coming into the room, her skinny legs propelling her forward in an awkward, stuttering stride.

"Sorry...." he said, wondering why the room had gone silent.

"How refreshing," said Ms. Danielpoor, "to see a man who knows when to apologize to a woman," she added, as she flipped open the satchel on her shoulder and emptied its contents onto her desk. "You don't see that every day — unless there's food, pay or sex involved. Which is it this time, Mr. Dixon?"

"How about stupidity?" said Derek, his face flushing.

"Good answer," said his teacher. "It seems Mr. Dixon is a feminist."

"Or just feminine," whispered a wise guy in the back of the room. But by then, the gaunt teacher was busy chalking up the blackboard with her florid script.

"What an idiot," muttered Derek, slumping down in his chair. Yet as Ms. Danielpoor began her discussion of Shakespeare's *A Midsummer Night's Dream*, Derek felt a gauze-covered hand patting him on the back. Though he looked up right away, Lena's eyes were already facing forward.

Sitting up, Derek wondered what made humans so changeable. One minute, Lena was insulted, the next sympathetic. Why would a species drenched in emotion since before they emerged from the forest still have so little self-control a million years later?

All the same, Earth people seemed aware of the problems caused by their undisciplined minds. This work of ancient theater was only one example. Of course, for Derek, the nuances of Elizabethan English were even more of a struggle than for the other kids in the class.

Sure, the Galactic Array's limitless powers of translation at least made it easy to follow along, but many aspects of the story made no sense to him. What did he know of human mating rituals, mythology or religion? Were the "faeries" vestiges of an extinct hyperspatial species?

The class bell sliced a deep gash through Derek's daydreams; he now had barely enough time to scribble down the homework assignment from the blackboard. Forced to keep up appearances, by writing down data he could access mentallically on the Array, he wondered how much longer he could bear up. This wasn't living; his days revolved around surviving undetected.

So as he glanced over at Lena, he realized he'd have to try harder to connect to the humans around him.

"I ... I didn't get to finish my thought, before," he said, wondering why his face felt so hot.

"Want to go for lunch?" asked Lena, her voice now the most soothing sound he'd heard in days.

"Sure," said Derek, scooping up his notebook and his copy of the *Kramden Anthology*.

"Don't take it the wrong way," said Lena, "I need help carrying my tray is all," she added, waving her gauzy hands.

"What wrong way?" asked Derek.

"You're a cute kind of clueless," she said and, stranger still, it sounded like a compliment.

Confused, he now saw that understanding sentient life from a distant galaxy was a long-range project. Even with the help of the Galactic Array, he'd need more than intellect. He'd have to feel his way into human interactions and, harder still, learn how to interpret conflicting human emotions.

Take Lena, for example. Far from being upset with Derek, she now seemed to enjoy his company; that was good enough for him. Better to leave "understanding" for another time.

Yet, as they chatted down the hall, he found it impossible to take his own advice. Only a few feet from the classroom door, Derek caught a glimpse of Callie Ann making out with "Blade" Northrop in a dark stairwell and went into mental overdrive.

What hold did this muscular guy with a permanent case of five o'clock shadow have over her? It wasn't his hygiene. Even Derek's new, weak human sense organs had no trouble detecting the stench of body odor, cigarettes and incense that seemed to ooze out of Blade's every pore.

But, as the author of the ancient stage play had known, love didn't have to "make sense" to be love or ... whatever Callie Ann felt for this smelly lug. Then again, what would Shakespeare have called Derek's feelings for her?

"What does she see in him?" Derek said at last.

"Who?" asked Lena.

"Forget it," said Derek, kicking a piece of wadded up notebook paper out of his way. "I better mind my own business."

"Good plan," said Lena, as they entered the cafeteria, whose jarring decor was a riot of turquoise and tropical orange. To Derek, the decor meant nothing; he had nothing to compare it to. For her part, Lena no longer gave it a thought. She was focused on the shimmering row of desserts waiting at the end of the line: bowl after bowl of her favorite lime Jell-O.

"Grab an extra one for me, will you?" she asked, pointing at two bowls on the far left.

Totally confused, Derek put one of the dessert bowls on his own tray, even though the thought of eating ... that ... was disgusting.

"You do know what they make this out of, don't you?" he asked, only to come face to face with Lena's bandaged left palm.

"Keep it to yourself," said Lena, as they shuffled across the polished vinyl tiles. "Lime Jell-O is my fave," she added, without mentioning it was also the last dessert Mom ever made.

Before long, Lena's obsession with hydrolyzed animal collagens had slipped from Derek's mind. He was too caught up with sitting around a cafeteria table with Lena and a few of her friends — one of whom was Vance Maultsby, now sporting a gray knit cap shoved down tight over his dark, wiry hair.

Across from him sat Celia Roberts, bragging to Lena about the way she'd "played" her parents. And there was Vance, arguing with Jeremy Leitner about the possibility of time travel. In spite of himself, Derek couldn't help smiling — hearing these two guys talk about space-time as if it were a road they could zoom down in a shiny chrono-car.

All the same, Derek discovered in his new friends something he never expected. Reading between the lines of the passive mentallic data he received from each of them, a pattern emerged.

Though none were telepathic, in small groups, their minds began working in sync, creating a latent mentallic community just below their consciousness. Yes, he nodded, he'd seen on the Array that the humans were aware of the phenomenon in a distant sort of way, referring over and over again to the "bonding" experiences that brought them together or the tendency of loved ones to finish each other's thoughts in conversation.

And yet nothing recorded on the Galactic Array prepared him for what he saw in Lena's mind: faint traces of another mentality left by a recent visit to her cerebral cortex. How could that be?

"You spacing out again?" Vance called out, smacking Derek on the side of the head.

"Sorry," said Derek. "I guess that's just what I do."

"Well cut it out," said Lena with a fake scowl. "People might think you're — you know — an alien."

"Yeah, like whoo-whoo-whoo-whoo-whoo-ooo, the aliens are coming," said Vance, raising his voice to a high falsetto.

Derek's spine stiffened as Lena and everyone else at the table joined in. Soon kids across the whole cafeteria picked up the sound and it echoed in waves to the exposed beam ceilings.

"Whoo-whoo-whoo-whoo-whoo-ooo," they chanted, until the class buzzer sounded, sending them scrambling into the hallway.

"That was cool," said Vance, shoulders shaking until he fell off his chair.

And for the first time since his arrival, Derek was thankful the Snaldrialooran Transmog Team had given him such a convincing replica of human physiognomy. Because underneath that outburst of manic glee he had clearly sensed a layer of deep-seated, violent fear.

CHAPTER TEN

Limping out of Gym class later in the day, Derek wondered how a civilization capable of rudimentary space flight could rely on such non-scientific methods to promote physical health. Without bothering to dredge up the relevant files on the Galactic Array — he was way too exhausted for that — he tried to work up an explanation based on his own observations.

Opening his mind a bit wider to the river of mentallic data pouring out of classmates, teachers and staff members, Derek found a confusing tangle of anxiety knotted around the concept of "fitness." Jammed up next to it were three nearly identical clusters around "manliness," "sexiness," and "wholesomeness."

And yet, noticing how his calf and thigh muscles began to stretch out as he walked down to the Computer Science lab, he had to admit the ritualized practice the humans referred to as "exercise" must have an intuitive basis in science. It was, he realized, a good feeling to survive a tough workout. But that was only part of the picture: a portrait of the human heart and mind at its deepest levels.

What, for example was the root of this human obsession with physical appearance? On the Homeworld, people were what they were physically and nothing was said about it, unless it posed a public health threat. Otherwise, individual variation was taken for granted and no one ideal of perfection had ever taken hold.

Not that fads for certain genetically inherited traits never broke out. That happened at least once a generation — but was quickly and quietly suppressed. Direct genomic remapping was also under strict administrative control. Any call in the Galactic Legislature to deregulate it was silenced with a recounting of the disaster on Djerloornatriva 7.

Some 200 years ago, the story went, unregulated genetic manipulation had split the planet's population into nearly a dozen incompatible species — some with predatory tendencies. In the chaos that followed, the dominant sentient culture collapsed, leaving millions of unmodified Djerloornatrivians at the mercy of millions more disease-ridden mutants. As a result, the planet had been closed to interstellar contact ever since, monitored remotely by satellite-mounted sensors.

Such horror stories aside, the innately telepathic Snaldrialoorans defined their "personal best" in terms of qualities of the mind that would be lost on humans. That, sighed Derek, was one more thing that made his frantic fascination with Callie Ann so incomprehensible.

Knowing the shape of her mind — like most human mentalities, a wild, impulsive tangle of fluctuating desires — he could only wonder what the fascination was. Even compared to other humans close to his own age, Callie Ann's thought processes seemed particularly scattered. That is, except when it came to swimming and related athletic activities.

Now, compared to oafish Gary Reynolds, Callie Ann's mind was a model of elegant order. Shuddering, Derek recalled the brief flashes of Gary's mind he'd glimpsed over the past two weeks: A swamp of obsessive spirals, most of which revolved around cheeseburgers, bodily functions and reruns of *Jackass*.

And then there was Lena, with qualities of mind he'd seen in no other Earth creature. What were the origins of her simultaneous passion for marine biology and metallurgy?

To find out, he realized, he'd need to make a thorough analysis — which the neurosuppressors in his wrist prevented him from carrying out. Yet despite the lack of hard data, Derek's intuition told him there was no connection between the unusual contours of Lena's mind and her recent brush with an alien mentality. Whatever impact the fungus had made on her, Lena's special qualities were hers alone. For the moment, she was fine — but Derek still felt uneasy, knowing the mystery might reveal itself at any moment.

By arriving early for Computer Science, he'd hoped to have a moment alone with the humans' ingenious, if primitive, leptonic communications network. Maybe he'd be lucky enough to find data confirming or denying the presence of an extra-terrestrial visitation — other than his own. But he was in for a surprise.

"Alien Dude," shouted Vance in a quivery voice as Derek walked in. Before Derek had time to blink, Vance had bounded across the room from a work station in a far corner and clapped hard him on the shoulder. Hard enough, that is, to make Derek wonder if his collar bone had popped out of its socket.

"Why are you here so early?" asked Derek, fighting hard not to show his disappointment.

"Dude, you can't keep me out of Computer Lab," said Vance, grinning. "I got a thing for programming. Come here, I wanna show you something...."

Pushed along by Vance's large, bony hands, Derek stopped in front of a display screen crammed with incomprehensible code.

"What does it do?" asked Derek, tilting his head to one side.

Manic glee burned in Vance's eyes as he described the video game he was developing, drawing data from Google Earth to build an interactive environment based on where players live.

"I don't even know if it'll work," said Vance, pushing his horn-rimmed glasses back to the bridge of his nose. "Mr. Lee — the other CompSci teacher? — thinks I'm wasting my time, but I think I'm OK if I make everything happen outside. And Mrs. Grant thinks I should go for it. Only thing is, I can't get the maps to sync up fast enough."

"How long will it take to build your ... game?" asked Derek, squeezing his face into a grimace. As a member of a stern, ancient race with rigid social protocols, people played games only in private; the public display of entertainment by humans was flat-out astonishing.

"You're seriously weird," said Vance, jumping out of his chair. "This is fun, don't you get that?"

"Settle down, boys," a calm voice cut in. The voice belonged to Mrs. Grant, who had just walked in with a rumpled raincoat slung over one arm. "Mr. Maultsby, close up your files and help me set up for class. That was the deal, right?"

"Right," said Vance with a sneer at Derek.

"And you, Mr. Dixon," she added, "It's not nice to rain on your friend's parade."

"Sorry," said Derek. Looking down at his Air Jordans, he wondered what impact atmospheric precipitation could possibly have on Vance's computer program. More to the point, were his new sneakers cool enough to impress Callie Ann?

CHAPTER ELEVEN

The following Saturday morning, Lena turned over in bed for the fifth time in half an hour. Between her fidgety legs and the way her nose kept whistling, "sleeping-in" was starting to feel like torture.

Better to get up and get far away from the stupid nightmare that had pestered her all night. Really. How many dorky things could happen in one dream? Who runs into the center of town, naked? And who has a shouting match with a mailbox?

Maybe her dreams were a side effect of the nasty medication the doctors had given her. According to Dad, they'd been worried enough to try an experimental therapy. Of course, all the nurse would say was that she'd been infected by a rare bacteria. That, Lena realized, was because she had been in the Children's Ward, where Bert and Ernie kept scary news away from little girls.

But since Mom died, Lena doubted any other scary news could trouble her much. That is, unless Dad....

OK, this was way too gloomy for a lazy Saturday morning when she had the whole house to herself. Dad was busy driving Rhea Silber back to Harmony Beach, so she could pack up her flower shop for the summer and head back to Boston for — whatever she did during the year. Lena hadn't had the chance to catch more than a few details of Rhea's life before the fungus incident flung Lena into a coma.

What was up with that fungus, anyway?

The doctors told Dad it had latched on to her central nervous system — giving her hallucinations. Her story about an airship crashing and burning into the Atlantic? Only a delirious rant.

"What would Bert and Ernie say about that?" Lena muttered. Yet, as sure as she was slipping into her favorite pair of flip-flops, she knew what she'd seen — and it was totally real.

Shuffling into the kitchen for breakfast, Lena replayed the last three weeks in her mind: The sonic boom, the mysterious envelope, the awful gunk it left on her hands, the three episodes of fainting or near-fainting — and strange little Derek. Not to mention strange little Derek's mom, a woman so beautiful and so ... so ditsy at the same time.

Forget it. Lena was hungry enough to eat a pack of wolves, for no reason she could come up with. It wasn't like she was starving herself. In fact, her distorted reflection in the microwave definitely told her the opposite.

Fine. She'd start on a diet today, maybe just have yogurt and fruit and then go for a run. She had no choice: the chances of finding another guy like Silvano were practically zero....

The bell on the toaster snapped her out of her daydreams.

"Oh, yeah, Reality," said Lena. "Thanks for reminding me."

Munching on the English muffin she'd found too hard to resist, Lena wondered how long she should wait until she went out jogging. Jogging! Why was she ... what was driving her to....

No, it couldn't be Derek, even if he was kind of a sweet guy. The uncomplaining way he'd helped her with her lunch tray and that funny habit of breaking into long, scientific lectures, made him ... well, what was it: strangely cute or cutely strange?

But it couldn't be him, even if he did have a nice smile and that unexpected fire in his eyes. It was like he could read your mind, the way he'd catch something for you, before you even knew you were dropping it....

Lena smacked her forehead. Why not focus on the important things, like the fact that her doctor had rewrapped her bandages yesterday, so she could use her fingers again? Weird how the trouble in your life made you thankful for small things.

Mind racing, she flipped on the radio. Maybe she could find some cool music. Too bad her favorite station was blaring out the news instead:

"... allegations that the sudden increase in the number of mailboxes in New Jersey and eastern Pennsylvania is part of a make-work program were vigorously denied by Winton Cragsmore, Postmaster General."

The Postmaster was not amused.

"What we're dealing with is a well-financed group of pranksters, going after cheap thrills at the expense of the American people...."

Lena almost burned herself on the toaster. "Pranksters," the angry political appointee had said. Wasn't that long ago she'd imagined herself a prank victim. But, come on, she told herself, pretty soon, the director of a dumb reality show would claim credit for the mailboxes.

No surprise there. The surprising part was, even spacey Derek knew about them.

Derek. Ever since that day on Harmony Beach, her mind kept circling back to the new kid who seemed so out of touch. Only yesterday, she'd seen him struggle with the zippers on his backpack — as if backpacks were a brand new concept. And how had he vented his frustration?

"I'm surprised the co-efficient of friction is so high along the outer edges of this pack."

Worse, he seemed to think this was normal conversation. Had he spent his life in an elite prep school for science geeks?

"Kind of sad," Lena muttered, grabbing an egg carton from the fridge. Soon enough, the sizzle of eggs in a frying pan eased her mind away from the present. It was such a relief to feel normal again. And as she slid the scrambled mass onto a plate, her mind sailed back over four years to an image of Mom serving up a big Saturday breakfast for Lena and her three sleepover friends — like it was nothing.

"But it wasn't nothing, was it?" said Lena to her mostly white cat with a black spot on his side that looked like....

"Arkansas! It wasn't nothing, was it, Baby?" she said, leaning down to scratch the fuzzy ears that were slinking past. How much, Lena wondered ... the way Mom exerted herself ... how much had that weakened her heart? If Lena hadn't been so needy....

Digging into her scrambled eggs, Lena wiped her eyes on her upper arm. As much as the guilt hurt, she realized, it also had its advantages. Blaming Mom's early death on herself gave it a comforting rational basis — even if that was self-destructive.

Not least because it was a beautiful fall morning and out through the window to her right, Lena could almost see the leaves of her neighbor's Japanese maple getting brighter and brighter. Off in the distance, a lawn mower was shooting the odor of cut grass into the morning air, making the kitchen smell fresh and alive.

But what was up with Arkansas? He'd barely budged in the last five minutes. Peering under the kitchen table, Lena could see his body tense, his tail droop and his ears flick backwards as he stared at the front door.

"Aarkyeee," she squeaked at him, in a high-pitched voice, "Aarkyeee, come here to me, Baby." But all she got for her trouble was a weird, angry "Merleow" and a streak of furry lightning that dashed out of the kitchen and galumphed upstairs.

Before Lena could wonder what had turned her placid Tom cat into a crouching tiger, she heard a faint tapping on the door to the back porch. Reaching for the bathrobe she'd slung over the back of her chair, Lena drew herself to her full 5'5'' and went to the door. Probably a jerk trying to sell her life insurance.

But the figure at the door wasn't a sales rep.

"Hi, Lena, Dear," said Mrs. Dixon, with a warm maternal smile. Of course, Lena had no way of knowing that this smile had been created by a flotilla of nanobots that worked the micropneumatic pathways under the robot's skin. "I hope I'm not interrupting your breakfast."

Trying not to gasp, Lena smiled back. Yet without the aid of nanobots, her smile wasn't quite so convincing.

"Mrs. Dixon?" she said. "Is everything OK?"

"Of course, Dear," said the impossibly sunny voice. "May I come in for a moment?"

Unable to resist, Lena motioned her in — though not before glancing through the threshold to see if anyone were watching. Standing alone with Mrs. Dixon's perfectly symmetrical face, she closed her eyes and tried to steady her breathing. Who drops in on Saturday morning without....

"I probably should have called first," said Mrs. Dixon, smiling. "But Derek was getting so frantic."

"Is he ... is he sick?" Lena suggested, hoping to move the conversation into more familiar territory. But instead, the situation kept getting weirder. As the startlingly beautiful woman explained, Derek had wanted to invite Lena over for lunch.

"He didn't know the correct courtesy protocol, and was afraid you'd be offended."

So, thought Lena, the solution was to send his mom? And, by the way, who talks like this? Maybe if Derek's mom had been 90 years old or had a foreign accent — any accent — it might have made sense. But, OK, it figured strange little Derek would have eccentric parents. Trouble was, Lena was starting to think the word "eccentric" made Mrs. Dixon sound way too normal.

"Tell him ... tell him to call next time," said Lena.

"So you won't come over?" asked Derek's mom. "Derry will be crushed. It has been so hard for him to make friends."

No surprise there, sighed Lena. But, realizing a visit to Derek's house was probably inevitable — now that he knew the correct "courtesy protocol" — she agreed to drop by at one o'clock. Having shown Derek's robotic mom to the door, she stood in the doorway, again marveling at Mrs. Dixon's graceful, gliding walk and the effortless way she slid into her quartz-blue Mercedes sedan, then drove out into the street on the perfect trajectory.

After waving goodbye, Lena closed the door and slumped back against it, letting the tension run out of her torso and down into the kitchen's fake terra cotta tiles. From upstairs, Arkansas' big padded feet brought him galumphing down into the kitchen and straight over to her ankles.

"Hi, Aarkyeee," said Lena, reaching down to scoop him up into her arms, "you being more friendly now?" And looking into the Tom cat's yellow-green eyes, Lena had the distinct impression that Arkansas was relieved Mrs. Dixon was gone. Come to think of it, Lena was, too.

CHAPTER TWELVE

Long about 11:30 that same morning, a dark figure skulked toward the Skudderton bus terminal, passing empty lots, stepping over broken concrete slabs — with the stub of a cigarette clinging to his lips. The lanky boy paused to peer into a crack in the plywood fence surrounding an abandoned building project, before clomping out toward the gray warehouse behind the main post office on Trolley Lane.

Pulling up the collar of his jean jacket against the early autumn chill, Blade Northrop felt the back of his throat fill with a splash of bitter liquid.

Most days, self-confidence ran in his veins. He never needed to psyche himself up to ask a girl out, bluff his way into a party or work over his teachers with one of his patented hard-luck stories. But this morning, as he steadied himself for his appointment with Mr. Yarrow, Blade felt his swagger sinking fast into his deep brown snake-skin cowboy boots.

They were the boots Chad Northrop had bought for him last summer on their trip to Nashville — the day before Chad's big meeting with Jimmy "Cooker" Morton. Even though Chad's only Top-Ten hit, *Hurtin' You,* had been out of print for years, Jimmy had audacious plans. He was eager to find out if igniting a Chad Northrop Comeback Tour would set his own career on fire.

Trouble was, Chad never could make it up before noon, not even for a life-changing 10:00 a.m. appointment. So now all that was left of Chad Northrop's dreams was a pair of dusty, scuffed and coffee-stained boots stomping up the ruined back steps of the Skudderton post office. And though Blade was glad he still remembered his trip to Nashville, he was starting to wish that, this time, he'd remembered to stay home.

"Time to man up," muttered Blade as he scratched his heels against a walkway patched together from jagged scraps of plywood.

Besides, what was the big deal? It wasn't like this Yarrow dude could force him to "join the team" as the intense entrepreneur kept repeating. But the money ... the money was too good to ignore. After one week, he'd have enough cash to get Chad's guitar out of hock — and after two weeks, enough to take Callie Ann up to New York for a long weekend of ... sightseeing.

Blade gasped as the sheet metal door he was planning to knock on swung open by itself. Mr. Yarrow peered out at him from inside a dark blue, hooded jumpsuit of crushed velvet.

"Get in," Yarrow growled.

Blade's boots clomped behind the wiry, middle-aged man, who led him around a labyrinth of steel plated dividers — left, right, left, left, right — until at last they entered the main sorting room of the Skudderton post office.

The usually cool Blade was shocked by what he saw: the hole blasted through the back of the building, to which this ramshackle warehouse had been added. Why hadn't anyone in Skudderton noticed? No wonder mail delivery had ground to a halt. And yet, as near as Blade could tell, he was the first guy in town to see the cause for himself.

Without a word of explanation, grim Mr. Yarrow motioned Blade to sit across from him at a round metal table, which looked like he'd bought it at an auction of B-movie scenery from the 1950s.

"The work is easy," said the small, but strangely imposing figure swathed in crushed velvet, "and the pay is good, especially for a lazy boy like you."

"Check the insults," said Blade, managing to keep his voice steady despite his pounding heart. "You know what? I'm out of here," he added, standing up. But before the muscular teenager could blink, Mr. Yarrow's hand snapped forward, grabbed Blade's forearm and held it tight.

"Sit. Listen," he said, his mouth drawn into a taut, red line. Ordinarily, Blade Northrop wasn't one to follow orders; at least, that's what he told himself. But this man's intense black eyes were overwhelming. Caught for a moment in Mr. Yarrow's stare, Blade couldn't shake how much they resembled the eyes of a wild beast. Feeling a sickening heat worm its way up his arm, Blade sat down again as his own eyes grew accustomed to the darkness around him.

In what had originally looked like an empty warehouse, Blade could now make out the distinct profile of machinery, as if the warehouse were a factory. What was that, over there in the corner.... Were they making mailboxes in here?

Mr. Yarrow wasn't saying. Not that Blade would dare ask. Besides, the last thing he wanted was to spend more time talking to a creepy guy in a dark blue crushed velvet jump suit. All he needed to know was that delivering a few packages a week was going to earn him enough money to leave Skudderton for good.

As he shuffled away from the dank warehouse and back down the sidewalk toward the center of town, Blade wondered if he should have asked more questions. Who the heck was this Yarrow guy and what had he done to the post office? Yet, as Blade counted his advance money, the snap of the green, crisp bills felt like the only answer he'd ever need. He was still counting when Callie Ann called on his cell. Crap. He was *supposed* to meet her at the Skudderton Y after swim team practice.

"Be right there, Babe," Blade crooned into his phone. "Had some mopping up to do for my dad ... You know what I mean."

Smiling, Blade Northrop hung up and looked up at the high vaulted ceiling the early fall sky had made. As the clouds floated by, he realized he had a talent for lying so profound he could probably take it on the road and make himself millions.

Except, that is, with Mr. Yarrow. No way you could lie to that dude.

It was like ... like he could read your mind. Good thing Callie Ann couldn't. There was a whole lot of stuff Blade didn't want her finding out. As it was, she wouldn't have found out half of what she did know — if it weren't for her fat-assed girlfriend. He'd have to keep his eye on Lena, he decided. If he could catch her out, he'd have something to hold over her head the next time she felt like telling Callie Ann what his girlfriend definitely did not need to know.

Funny how Mr. Yarrow already knew about Lena. He'd even showed Blade a snapshot of her on a weird-looking tablet, which looked to Blade like it must have been made in Japan. Blade couldn't imagine Lena meeting anyone like Mr. Yarrow in her entire life. But what had Blade's new boss said, exactly?

"You know this girl," asked the dark beady eyes peering out from under the hood of his jumpsuit. "This Lena?"

"What about it?" asked Blade, covering his fear with a mask of indifference.

"Just stay clear of her," said Mr. Yarrow, tapping the tablet's touch screen. "That's all I'm saying," he added, as if they were comparing notes on the best place to get sushi. Trouble was, everything Mr. Yarrow said sounded deadly serious and, Blake realized, the "deadly" part was what counted most.

CHAPTER THIRTEEN

Riding over to Derek's house in the Hunter's Wend section of Skudderton, Lena peered through her visor and tried to make sense of the images whirling past. As Dad's forest green Vespa Milano scooter purred around the bends in the road, she couldn't help noticing subtle changes in the style and quality of the homes, the closer she got to Derek's semi-exclusive neighborhood.

"They must have some serious money," she muttered.

Still, with the cool air streaming across her face, the faint twinge of envy in her mind was soon dissipated. Leaning into the next curve, Lena realized she had everything she wanted and, most of the time, more than she needed. That is, except for ... for Mom ... but more money couldn't make up that deficit anyway.

What *was* disturbing were the odd clumps of mailboxes cropping up every hundred yards or so. There! On the left at the next stoplight, she counted no fewer than five at the same corner, packed together in such a wild cluster there was hardly room to walk past them. As the traffic light changed, Lena decided they looked like an assortment of mushrooms, springing up after a rain shower.

But what was the deal with that bright yellow one? Pulling over to the curb for a closer look, she squinted at the writing on the front panel. What language was it ... was that German, maybe?

Yet the seriously weird part was, each time she neared a clump of mailboxes she felt as if she were in a crowded airport, like the one she was in with Dad when they saw Aunt Kathy off to Vancouver last April.

Could be, she figured, a gardener was doing grounds work nearby with the radio on. Or maybe it was nerves. Heading over to Derek's for lunch after his mom popped in unexpectedly? It was enough to rattle anybody.

"So why go?" she asked the scraggly gray cat racing across the road at the next intersection. It could only be because, Lena knew, Derek was a strange kind of different — maybe even different enough to be....

Gunning the Vespa as hard as she dared in this sedate part of town, Lena shook her head.

"He's not like Silvano at all, and you know that," she mumbled. And yet, she realized, he didn't *need* to have anything in common with her faraway boyfriend. Strange little Derek might turn out to be a nice guy to hang out with once in a while. For now, that was enough. Later, maybe, once the Callie Ann Effect had worn off a bit....

Wait. Wasn't that Blade Northrop in his dad's cherry red Malibu? What was he doing in this neighborhood? Whatever, Lena decided to put her curiosity to good use. If she tailed Blade long enough, she might catch him acting out; she'd have the evidence to make Callie Ann see what a dangerous loser he was.

It would take her out of her way, but big deal. Derek could wait a few minutes. A girl had to look out for her friends, especially a friend like Callie Ann, who was pretty enough to have boys interested in her for every wrong reason.

There, Blade was stopping. Sizing up the terrain quickly, Lena figured she could pull over to the shoulder, and hide in the shade of that big willow tree up ahead. Besides, with Dad's Darth Vader-ish helmet on, she doubted Callie Ann's dim bulb of a boyfriend would recognize her.

Lena held her breath and watched as the tall, scruffy boy took a large package out of the trunk of his car and lugged it over to a clump of mailboxes on the northeast corner of the street. Having set it down, he dug a set of keys out of his jacket pocket and unlocked the largest of them: a bright red box with what looked like Chinese characters embossed in white on the front.

Things got weirder. Even though the obviously foreign mailbox was only about a third of the size of the package, Blade still managed to get the whole thing inside, with room to spare. The moment Blade had opened the mailbox's front panel, Lena froze, as the echoing sounds of a crowded airport she'd heard before grew louder and louder — but cut off immediately, as soon as Blade slammed the box shut.

Shuddering as a cool breeze whipped up around her, Lena forced herself to sit still until Blade was back in his car and zooming up the street ahead of her. Though, realistically, saying Chad Northrop's car could "zoom" was a bit of a stretch.

When the sound of the Malibu's cracked muffler was only an echo on the horizon, Lena finally felt comfortable enough to ease her scooter out of the shadows and back up the street toward Derek's gated community. Wait, was that her cell phone?

"Hey, Lena ... you coming over?" Derek's slightly hoarse voice crackled into her ear.

"Be there soon," said Lena, hanging up before he had a chance to ask questions. With only a short distance left to go, she figured she needed every second to come up with a plausible excuse for being late. She certainly couldn't tell Derek the truth.

Besides, what had she really seen? Was this like whatever she'd seen on the *Shari Lynn* — a hallucination no one would believe? As if in answer, the same echoey crowd sounds flared up in her mind again. And for one brief moment, she could swear she heard a voice laughing. Not the low, maniacal laugh of an "Evil Genius" in one of Silvano's cheesy horror movies. No, it sounded more like the mocking jeer of a sassy, nine-year-old girl.

Turning into Derek's driveway at last, Lena snapped off her helmet and tried to catch her breath. For now, the voices in her head had stopped. But deep down, she knew: Like the painful, itchy stiffness she'd felt in her palms, the sounds would be sure to return. The sensations they brought with them were way too familiar to ignore.

CHAPTER FOURTEEN

Earlier that same Saturday morning, Ixdahan Daherek sat up, smashed his palm down on his squawking clock radio and listened to the enveloping silence. With any luck, he hadn't roused the two DXN units from their recharging stations.

Peering into darkness, he slid out of bed and left his room for the upstairs hallway. At three a.m., it was still five hours before DXN/SRH would interrupt Lena's breakfast, eight and a half hours before Blade Northrop would meet Mr. Yarrow and three hours before Todd Gabrilowicz would slip into his Touareg with Rhea Silber — his head full of plans for the future.

Now at the top of the stairs, Ixdahan eased himself down into the living room a step at a time. Stairs were still a bit of a problem. First, his depth perception would fail. Then the painful creaking in his knees would begin, the result, he'd read, of a transient inflammation afflicting many human adolescent males. Or had the Transmog Team made his kneecaps half a size too small?

The pain was worth it.

Because only now, when the robots were dormant, could the former heir to L'han Singha Province regain control of his own mind. Not that his mind was unchanged. His hours of agony in the transmog chamber and his time on Earth had given him a fresh perspective. Instead of wealth, power and social status, the one thing he prized was a few minutes alone with his true thoughts.

That is, unless he counted his conversations with Lena or the slightest glimpse of Callie Ann's green eyes. Was it a global human failing or a flaw in his *own* character? There was no way to know. But while Lena's company gave him confidence, even courage, it was Callie Ann who dominated his mind.

Derek flinched at the chime of the antique grandfather clocks DXN/SRH had insisted were a culturally mandated living room accessory. The DXN units would be fully charged in less than four hours and the punishment for breaking the rules was the spine-searing pain of the *djalcrohloor*.

Sweat beaded up on the back of his neck, but he pressed on. Hold it ... were the DXN units stirring, or was that scraping sound the rustle of dry, autumn leaves in the night air?

Satisfied, Ixdahan tiptoed across the living room to the mantelpiece, where the robots' metadigital transponder now glittered briefly in the glare of a passing headlight. Would the transponder give him access to parts of the Galactic Array he couldn't reach on his own?

"Better had," he whispered into the shadows. The shiny device offered his only hope to answer a nagging question: Where had the traces of non-human intelligence come from that he'd detected on Wednesday? They pointed in only one direction.

For one thing, Ixdahan recognized their mentallic signatures. They were identical to the signals emitted by the "mutant mailboxes," clustered like weeds at his local bus stop. For another, the stray mentallic traces, though they had permeated the group consciousness of the entire school, had left their strongest mark on Lena's mind.

They also matched the maniacal mentality of Ambassador Ghaar, the Vrukaari official to whom Ixdahan had sold top secret documents only a few rotations ago. But how could he be sure?

Sighing, he realized for the hundredth time how much of his life he'd wasted, chasing after social dominance instead of getting a solid education. Maybe he could have found a way to break free from his metadigital jailers.

But, as Ixdahan also knew, the mistakes of his former life were not enough to account for his fuzzy thinking. As he'd already suspected in the lander, his DXN units *must* be equipped with powerful cortical dampeners. Fully charged, the robots created complex mentallic interference patterns — making it impossible for him to access every aspect of his consciousness.

Once the robots were reactivated, Ixdahan's mind would again be trapped in a spiral of feverish human emotion and impaired reasoning. He'd become "Derek," and have no hope of averting the crisis he sensed on the mentallic horizon.

Ironically, the only positive thing in the current situation was linked to something negative. The fall he'd taken when Gary Reynolds tripped him had damaged the neurosuppressors implanted in his left forearm. With effort, Ixdahan could now access more of his former telepathic abilities. But why hadn't his robotic jailers noticed? And, by the way, why hadn't they said a word about the mutant mailboxes?

Ixdahan gasped. Could the alien mentality he'd detected in the mailboxes have damaged the DXN units?

"That's it," said Ixdahan. "I have to try."

Despite the risk, he'd break every protocol of his exile and use the metadigital transponder to forge an active link to the deepest layers of the Galactic Array. With the transponder, he might be able to examine these stray mentallic traces more closely. And yet, if he were detected....

"Come on, you pathetic *balchriahnax*," he whispered. "Your ancestors are watching." With that, his mind burned hotter, brighter than ever before and ... got it!

Concentrating on the sector of the Array most likely to contain the shielded information he sought, he pushed every other thought from his mind.

Holding his breath, he drew on the skills that had helped him evade detection for months on the Homeworld, including secrets handed down through every generation of House Daherek. There wasn't a *janirge* to spare. Already, the twin robots were stirring to life as their power cells reached full capacity.

"System entry countermanded," said the Galactic Array's security AI. Worth a try, Ixdahan shrugged. Was it possible the security codes he'd used to break into the Ministry of Defense database were still operative? The security team would have to have been grossly incompetent not to close off the route he had taken — and yet, the Array was on the vast side of huge....

Sentient Masters of the Infinite Continuum, it worked!

Now, if he could break through to the most recent military briefings, he might find data to confirm or deny his worst fears: that the fungus he'd seen on Lena's hands originated offworld. But there were millions of files and no way to gauge the sheer volume of data streaming through his mind.

"Forget the odds," he whispered.

A mentallic screen of headlines appeared before him, hawking news items from the time since his ship had lifted off from the Homeworld. Ixdahan's forehead tensed as he tried to assess the relevance of each — including two headlines that stood out from the rest:

Vrukaari Acquire Level 6 Transmog
Technology; Informant Exiled.

and ....

Ambassador Ghaar Asserts
News of Vrukaari Strike Force,
Leaving Galaxy "Based on Faulty Data."

Breathing heavily, Ixdahan closed contact with the transponder and stared blankly around him as a smile traced itself across his lips. In this moment of happy exhaustion, a stray thought had wormed its way into his consciousness.

"I *could* try to contact Mother," he whispered into the shadows. It was seven cycles since the day she'd stormed out, flailing her tentacles and hurling curses at Pertahru.

Who could blame her? The sound of Father saying "Eneselah, be reasonable," in that dry, objective tone was enough to send anyone into a spiral of rage.

A glint of sunlight bounced off the glass-topped coffee table, driving that painful memory from his mind. Looking up, his heart raced as his eyes traced the path of the morning light through the living room's lace curtains. The *djalcrohloor*!

"Derek?" called George Dixon from upstairs. "What are you doing up, Boy? You know the rules."

Ixdahan braced himself. In the seconds remaining before his consciousness faded back into human form, he realized he'd have to bluff his way out.

"Couldn't sleep Dad," he yelled. Think! What was it Celia Roberts was bragging to Lena about in the cafeteria yesterday?

"They caught me red-handed," Celia had said, "So I did what I always do? Cried like a *baby*. Oh yeah. It works every time.... "

Looking up, Derek caught sight of the robot's stern face glaring down at him on the stairwell.

"What's this about, Son?" asked the DXN unit, his nanobots' micropneumatic pathways configuring themselves into a stern, paternal glare. "I figured a smart boy like you would remember the punishment for Rule Breakers."

"But Dad," said Derek, breaking into tears that weren't as fake as he meant them to be. "I hate my life! I don't have any friends — because I'm ... I'm too different. The transmog chamber didn't work right. It's so totally unfair!"

And in saying so for dramatic effect, Derek realized the truth of his own words. It *was* painful to be so different, so isolated! Dissolving into tears, he felt the full weight of his suffering for the first time.

"Now what's my baby crying about?" cooed Sarah Dixon as she glided down the stairs. Before he knew it, Derek was explaining how he'd wanted to invite Lena over for lunch, but didn't know enough about human customs. The emotional pain was worse than Derek had anticipated, no matter how warm and snuggly he felt in Sarah Dixon's robotic arms. But what was she saying now?

"I'll pay your friend a visit, Derry Dear, and we'll get everything arranged."

"Don't spoil the boy like that, Sarah," said George from the stairs, "Excessive Fraternization is against Protocol."

"Absence of Social Contact is a Category 1 Denoter, though, now isn't it George, Dear?" Derek's metadigital Mom shot back.

Derek marveled at the complex logic tree they traced as they weighed the outcome of each probability vector. At last, DXN/GRG relented.

"Your mom will drive over there first thing in the morning, Son," said George Dixon, his voice softening in discrete voltage increments. "Now get back to bed — and no more of your whining."

Trudging upstairs, Derek made them promise not to let him oversleep. There was something important he wanted to tell Lena, though he couldn't quite remember. All he knew was that, for once, it had absolutely nothing to do with Callie Ann.

CHAPTER FIFTEEN

With everything she'd seen since that scary August twilight out on the *Shari Lynn*, Lena found it hard to believe time kept flowing past her. Not that it made any sense, but she was secretly hoping a force of Nature would sit up and take notice. Yet right now, the only one sitting up was Derek, and he was on the edge of his seat. It was kind of cute — and kind of depressing — to see how far he craned his neck for a better view.

From the way he gawked, you'd think every member of the swim team was wearing a thong bikini instead of a one-piece team uniform. Not that these girls weren't graceful and trim, Lena realized, glancing down at her own torso.

"No competition," she whispered.

At least she'd had the good sense to wear black, she told herself. Yet, despite the tinge of jealousy clouding her mind, the sight of the girls varsity swim team in action made the third week of the term reassuringly normal. Now if she could get Derek to stop squirming in his seat.

"You feeling OK?" she asked him, suppressing the urge to feel his forehead.

"Just nervous," said strange little Derek. "Gary Reynolds has been giving me dirty looks ever since I got off the bus."

Lena bit her lip. Either this guy was completely out of touch with reality or totally naive. Not that one option ruled out the other. But if she had any thought of challenging Derek, the shrill tweet of the referee's whistle knocked it right out of her head. The first heat of swimmers was lining up and, she realized, nothing short of a nuclear blast could pry Derek away from the view.

Where was Callie Ann? As Captain, even when it wasn't her heat, she was usually right at the edge of the pool, clapping and shouting to keep her teammates psyched. No surprise Derek was disappointed, though why he expected Lena to have the answer for everything was beyond her. Turning around to Vance Maultsby, who was sitting behind her, one row up, she asked:

"You see Callie Ann anywhere down there?"

Vance grinned and nodded at Derek. "Nope," he said. "What? You crushing on her too, now? Aw, you know how it is,. She probably had a fight with what's-his-name. Oh, by the way...."

"Yeah?" asked Lena, wondering at the twinkle that now appeared in his eye.

"I heard Coach Roberts was gonna fill up the pool with lime Jell-O for you, but ... but Mr. Cosentino blocked it," said Vance, his voice breaking up into a loud cackle.

"You have a problem, you know that?' said Lena, slapping him across the knees. "I'm seriously worried about Callie Ann and all you can do is crack stupid jokes."

"OK ... Kay ... sorry," said Vance, fighting to catch his breath. "Hey, isn't that her now?"

And at the sight of Callie Ann strutting towards her team mates, the crowd of home team parents and students gave a rousing cheer. Among the loudest, Lena couldn't help noticing, was Derek, looking kind of cool in the clothes she'd helped him pick out for occasions like this.

"Must be out of my mind," she mumbled under the tide of reverberating whistles and claps. Because even though Derek was no closer to getting a date with Callie Ann, he was starting to look like "boyfriend material" for another girl, she feared, besides sort-of-OK-looking Lena Gabrilowicz.

At last, the cheering died down as the scoreboard cleared for the first event of the afternoon. And with it went Derek's enthusiasm. You'd have thought he was the birthday balloon a bratty kid's jealous older brother had stuck with a fork.

What was up with him?

He'd been like this on Saturday, too, when she'd stopped in for lunch. At first, he'd been his usual awkward self, getting way too flustered every time his syrupy mom corrected him — which happened about every five minutes. Meanwhile, Derek's dad turned out to be a non-stop geyser of folksy wisdom. Weirder still, neither parent ate more than a mouthful the whole time — though the table was piled with every type of classic comfort food.

Derek, on the other hand, had eaten like a lost soul returning from a month alone on a desert island. You'd almost think his parents kept him half starved. Or was it a case of nerves, she wondered — figuring this might well be the closest thing he'd ever had to a date?

Yet, once lunch was over and his parents had cleaned up with creepy, silent efficiency, Derek's mood had shifted into a dark, sullen sulk.

The rest of the afternoon, as they poured over the computer in Derek's room and Lena tried to explain "fashion sense" to him, she couldn't shake the feeling that he was on the verge of asking her a question. That is, not the usual guy stuff — that would have been almost a relief — but something more urgent.

Finally, after Lena had worn herself out Googling answers to Derek's minute questions about Armani jeans, he had looked up from the detailed notes he was taking on an iPad and stared at her a full minute.

"What?" yelled Lena, totally creeped out.

"When do you tell someone the truth?" asked Derek.

"Always," said Lena.

"But what if the truth were ... hard to accept?" asked Derek, sounding as if he'd aged 20 years.

"Then it depends on how you tell it," said Lena, nodding, remembering the day four years ago when Dad had to tell her about ... in the hospital....

The silence that answered her almost felt like a living presence. It was as if she could hear Derek thinking, but about what? The price of sneakers? Callie Ann? The price of Callie Ann's sneakers? After what felt like hours, Derek asked:

"You know anything about radios?"

Without waiting for an answer, he had taken her by the hand, led her downstairs to the living room, and stopped in front of the most high-tech — and probably the most expensive — radio she'd ever seen.

Gazing out the glass sliding doors leading to a half-acre plot of grass, Lena found herself envying Derek's parents, doing yard work with the same astonishing efficiency they'd shown when serving lunch.

But nothing Derek's parents did felt as weird as this moment, standing alone with Derek, holding her hand in front of what she assumed must be a new kind of satellite radio receiver. That is, except for the fact that Derek's hand, holding hers, was surprisingly soothing.

"My dad says this radio works perfectly," said Derek, pointing at the gleaming, stainless steel device. "But I can't hear a thing when I turn it on. You think I'm going deaf?"

"Dunno.... " Lena sputtered, wondering why he was asking her instead of his parents. Were they that hard to deal with?

"Feel like I'm going crazy," said Derek. "If I turn it on, would you tell me, honestly, if you hear anything?"

Lena nodded and, before she knew it, Derek had clicked a series of buttons at the top right of the sleek device. At first, it seemed as if nothing had changed. Slowly ... there it was ... a sound, a voice ... speaking in a language she was pretty sure couldn't possibly be human. And yet she understood every word.

Trouble was, those sounds couldn't be words, could they? It was like listening to a walrus with a cleft palate recite "The Star Spangled Banner" in Hindi. And yet....

"Interstellar Consortium," the voice was saying. "Interstellar Consortium convening today re: apparent Vrukaari incursion into the Remote Regions. Ambassador Ghaar recalled to Vrukaar Prime."

Lena's temples began to throb.

"Hear anything?" Derek asked, studying Lena's face.

"No," said Lena, her eyes fixed on the radio. "Nothing. I guess it's busted, like you said."

"Said I didn't know how to work it," said Derek. "But that doesn't matter ... if you didn't hear anything."

"Didn't," said Lena, facing him at last. "Want to take a break and try out my dad's Vespa?"

But Derek had waved her away and, with a flick of his fingers, shut off the device. Soon after, Lena scootered home, more worried than ever about the direction her life was taking.

Looking at him now in the bleachers surrounding the Skudderton Y's Olympic swimming pool, Lena recognized the same faraway look on Derek's face she'd seen on Saturday — as if he were not only thinking but listening to a conversation no one else could hear. Was he hearing the same voice she'd pretended not to hear on his father's radio? She was dying to ask him, but this was definitely not the time or place to tell him she was a liar.

Sliding down into her seat, Lena shook her head and tried to focus on the swim meet, marveling at how everyone around her could be oblivious to the confusion romping through her head like a clan of bonobos. With her shins pressed tightly into the back of the seat in front of her, she wondered how it was possible for the swimmers and the spectators to be having such a typical day — while she was busy going insane.

CHAPTER SIXTEEN

Late that night, as Derek slept, floating in a dream world of swimming pools, swimsuits and the swimmers in them, his two DXN units were deep in conversation. Like the mentallic exchanges they'd had every night of his exile, their thoughts spilled out as they lay, semi-conscious, in their precision-crafted recharging stations.

But tonight, instead of a neutral exchange of telemetry, their linked metadigital dataflow was noticeably distorted. Though you might think twice about calling their state of mind "anxious," you can bet a more precise description would fill several volumes of a textbook on artificial intelligence no one on Earth was liable to write for several centuries.

Despite having checked and rechecked their calculations with unerring precision, the two robots found they could not escape the inexorable conclusion: They were both in midst of a major malfunction.

It had begun imperceptibly, as the subtle poisoning of their memory circuits at first served only to shield the two robots from the unfolding Vrukaari plot. And so the appearance of the first mutant mailboxes went unnoticed, unrecorded in the Galactic Array they had gradually infected each time they accessed it to report on the exiled Snaldrialooran criminal in their charge.

Affecting DXN/SRH at first, it had spread to DXN/GRG a few weeks later, enough of a delay for George Dixon to enjoy only one brief moment more of heightened awareness.

"Memory seems less crisp than usual, now doesn't it?" he'd asked Sarah Dixon that night before entering the recharging station.

"Impossible," came the instantaneous reply, "my memory circuits are self-repairing, as are yours."

"Not if the repair units are packing a virus they're not," said Derek's robotic dad.

"Recommend powering me down to initiate full spectrographic analysis," said Sarah Dixon, her voice losing its carefully calculated illusion of human warmth.

"Can't rightly say I remember how," said George Dixon, slipping into his side of the recharging unit. There the matter rested, as the cumulative impact of the Vrukaari fungus spread from circuit to circuit, at first blinding their sensors to the truth and then blinding them altogether. Only as the cascading effects of the infection had begun to accelerate exponentially did emergency backup systems finally go online ... too late.

"Probability of metadigital dissociation now at 45% and climbing," said DXN/SRH through a thin veil of electromagnetic static.

At a later date, the log books of the Interstellar Consortium would trace the inception of decline to the moment an adolescent human female, infected with a Vrukaari fungoid, had touched the upper right lateral appendage of the damaged unit. In hindsight, the Consortium's eagerness to mimic the precise cellular composition of human skin had exposed the DXN units to the full force of the contaminant.

The results spoke for themselves as, slowly at first, but with geometric acceleration, the cyber-neuronic pathways of the robots' central processing units had been ruthlessly eroded.

" ... now at 50% and climbing.... " stuttered DXN/GRG, slurring his words as he shifted more and more of his memory circuits to the task of finding an antidote to the viral infection that was slowly eroding his memory circuits. Soon, the personality vectors of the two units collapsed, making their final transmissions impossible to assign to one or the other.

"Data suggests ... protein sequencing similar to...."

"Vru ... Vru...."

" ... kaar...."

" ... i...."

"dissociation at 88% and.... "

" ... 92 ... and.... "

CHAPTER SEVENTEEN

At 3:00 a.m. that morning, when Ixdahan jammed his thumb down on his alarm, he had no idea what had happened to his DXN units. Pacing at the foot of his bed, he listened deep into mentallic space for signs the robots' mental aura had resurfaced ahead of schedule.

Of course, if his suspicions about the Vrukaari were correct, waking a pair of metadigital AIs was not much of a risk.

As he sank down into one of two leather couches in his living room, Ixdahan searched his reintegrated mind for a solution. Free of the DXN-units' cortical dampening fields, he could calculate the impending probability curve in depressing detail: The Vrukaari war ministry would soon launch a full-scale invasion of Earth, using the transmog technology he had sold them for practically nothing.

"I did this," he whispered into the darkness.

The situation was probably more critical than it seemed. What if the invasion of Earth were only a dry run? If the test mission succeeded, the Vrukaari could use similar tactics on a much larger scale in his own galaxy. But as Ixdahan crept over to the metadigital transponder he'd told Lena was only a satellite radio, his heart told him there was another reason he had to take action.

When he was honest with himself, he knew he felt close to the friends he'd made in this hideous, transmogged body. The thought of Lena, Vance and Callie Ann becoming target practice for a slimy Vrukaari ground warrior was unbearable. Not even Gary Reynolds deserved such treatment — though his clothes did always smell of today's stale French fries and yesterday's rancid bacon.

Ixdahan pushed his head into his hands — and was startled to find them drenched by a flood of tears. Drying his hands on his T-shirt, he realized he'd not only betrayed his own people but all sentient life in two galaxies. If his friends — and Gary — were killed it would be the direct result of his crime.

His mind darkened. What could he do to save them? His attempt to warn the Homeworld the night before had come to nothing. Having broken through to the Interstellar Consortium, his conversation with the Snaldrialooran Secretariat of Defense had degenerated into a shouting match.

"Son of Pertahru!" Hiuch Minister Kalaarian Olthrat had thundered. "I will not participate in your unlawful attempt at communication with the Homeworld."

For his trouble, Ixdahan was now charged with a second count of treason, including a violation of the terms of his exile and an attempt to "distract and subvert the Secretariat of Defense."

At least Ixdahan had achieved part of his goal. The Snaldrialooran government had launched a new mission to Earth. But instead of a mandate to stop the Vrukaari invasion, the captain's orders were to arrest Ixdahan and bring him in for interrogation.

"Great," he muttered as he slapped his hands down on the coffee table. "I have to save an entire planet."

Trouble was, the irony of the situation offered him nowhere to hide. Even his conviction that the Vrukaari invasion plan was mind-bogglingly stupid gave him no comfort. As life had already taught him, there was no clear relationship between the relative stupidity of an idea and its likelihood to succeed.

All things being equal, Stupidity's subliminal link to the essential entropy of the universe gave idiocy on this scale a disturbing ring of plausibility. A strike force, 10 million-strong, disguised as street-level postal storage lockers? It could totally work.

Analysis complete, it was time to act. If he couldn't save his friends' entire species, he might at least be able to save his friends. Fortunately, his previous success in breaking through to the inner core of the Galactic Array had permanently fried the damaged neuro-suppressors implanted in his left wrist — so he could now send and receive mentallic energy at full force.

Pressing his palms together as he stood before the glowing metadigital transponder, Ixdahan focused his mind, hoping to make contact with the one person he knew might offer a solution. In fact, Ixdahan's older cousin Jalgren was probably the only mind on the Homeworld who'd be willing to speak to him at all. Jalgren had continued to send regular posts on the Galactic Array, including news of Ixdahan's mother, which his father, Pertahru, had repeatedly refused to share with him.

Besides, Jalgren Altrollinhar, distinguished Professor of Transgenomics at Lohar University, with an in-depth knowledge of Mutation-Matrix Theory, might also be the only Snaldrialooran with the skill to….

"Did you even think about how much trouble I'd be in if this transmission were overheard by the authorities?" snarled Cousin Jalgren, when Ixdahan had finally found his mentallic signal.

"Please," said Ixdahan, allowing the full force of his despair to broadcast itself, unshielded, across the spatio-temporal pathways of the Galactic Array. Sensing he'd piqued Jalgren's interest, Ixdahan proceeded to transmit every byte of data he'd collected since he'd first noticed the traces of an alien mentality in the mind of the young human female he now counted, incredibly, as his best friend.

To his relief, Cousin Jalgren came up with a plan of attack — one with the simplicity of genius and a surprise twist. It grew directly out of the realization that the Vrukaari, when it came to advanced technology, were far behind the curve. Far from innovators, they were scavengers, acquiring equipment by stealth, murder and, as in his case, bribery.

All the same, Ixdahan realized, Jalgren's attack plan was a long shot and, worse, by enlisting his human friends to save Earth, he'd be risking their lives.

As the transmission ended, and Ixdahan closed contact with his Homeworld, a glint of light in the corner of his eye brought his head up sharply.

Sunrise! Peering out the sliding glass patio doors leading off the living room, he realized he'd once again stayed too long at the transponder. But where was the deadening effect of the cortical dampeners on his mind? And where was George Dixon's booming voice of disapproval? Teeth clenched, he charged upstairs, hoping to reach his room before it was too late — only to find that the door to the robots' bedroom was unexpectedly ajar.

CHAPTER EIGHTEEN

Pulling the goggles tighter around her eyes, Lena hunched forward in her chair, lit the acetylene torch and flinched at its powerful blast of flame. Despite the leather gloves, leather apron and steel-toed work boots the school required, she couldn't shake the feeling she was handling a loaded gun.

"OK, focus," she whispered into her gloves.

Between this year and last, Ms. Dover had gone over the basics a million times. Unlike the confusing collection of weirdness she'd lived through since August, here in Metal Shop, things made sense.

Now, if she could keep the design clear in her head. Honestly, though? She was making it up as she went, searching her memory for shapes and textures that belonged together — and would add up to an object beautiful, stirring and mysterious.

On second thought, she had enough mystery in her life already. As she reached for a sheet of rusted metal stock, Lena shook her head at the latest twist. That morning at breakfast, Dad had greeted her with a shy smile.

"Got something to tell you, Lenaroo," he had said, getting up from his buttered wheat toast.

"Oh God, this about Rhea isn't it?" Lena had asked.

"Don't spoil the surprise," said Dad, pulling her into a big bear hug.

Todd Gabrilowicz and Rhea Silber were getting married.

Even now, hours later, Lena had to switch off her torch and wipe her eyes, without letting on. No good trying to convince your teacher you were up for welding — with tears streaming down your face. Lena couldn't afford to let Ms. Dover see her like this; she'd been looking forward to Metal Shop since June.

Trouble was, between normal drama, like Dad remarrying, and weird drama, like Derek being Derek, she barely had room in her brain to think her own thoughts.

Crowding her mind more than usual were the waves of babbling voices that had been crashing against her brain since that August twilight on the *Shari Lynn*. Only now, it was worse. Ever since she'd heard Derek's "radio," she could understand most of what the voices were saying.

Lena's jaw tensed as she remembered what she'd heard already. True, she had no ear for the nuances of the alien language, much less the culture that generated it, but she was clear on the main points. And they all revolved around Conquest.

What could that mean?

Had that weird fungus tuned her mind to an extra-terrestrial sports station? Could she be hearing an intergalactic team captain talking trash about his opponents? Maybe. But, as she relit the acetylene torch, Lena realized the tone the voices took wasn't anybody's idea of good-natured boasting. It had the unmistakable imprint of blood lust.

"C'mon, focus," she whispered again.

Aliens or no, Lena knew she had to finish her schoolwork, especially in a situation where no one could possibly take her seriously. Earth, the whole of human society, decimated by an army of mutated mailboxes? Better get some rest — preferably in a mental institution. And so Lena worked, nodding gratefully from time to time as she acknowledged the suggestions of Ms. Dover, a woman Lena envied for her air of gracious calm.

Little by little, the sculpture was taking shape. Yet, as she stood back to admire it in the last few minutes of class, her admiration was clouded over by a sickening thought: Lena's first major metalwork sculpture looked like the mailbox Blade Northrop had opened when she was on her way to Derek's house on Saturday.

Great, now the mailboxes and whatever was in them, were *completely* ruining her life. If she had any thought of making Dad and Rhea a wedding present out of metal, she'd have to start over. Maybe it was just as well. Looking down at her afternoon's work, she wondered if she'd also hear it muttering in her mind about "The Team," "The Plan" and "The Sub-Sentients."

And yet, for the moment, as she hurried to put away her tools and clean up, the mind-ways were quiet. She had, at last, enough space in her head to think about the surprise IM she'd had from Silvano the night before: His father's movie project in Milan had been canceled. He might be coming back to the States! As excited as she was by the possibility, his next entry brought her happiness crashing down:

"U have mutant mailboxes 2?" he'd typed.

The weirdness had finally struck Italy. Worse, when Lena tried to IM back a description of the crazy-strange events she'd dealt with since August, her account froze and her computer shut down, displaying five words in white characters against a blue background:

No one will believe you.

A sob choked Lena's throat as she imagined Silvano trapped in Italy while the world came apart — ensuring she'd never see him again. There had to be a way to keep him safe, but where could she turn for help? That's when it hit her: As much as she hated to admit it, saving the world might depend on putting her faith in the nerdy boy she had met only 18 hours after the second worst day of her life. It was a scary thought, but it seemed inescapable: wherever the mailboxes had come from, strange little Derek Dixon had come from, too.

Then, taking one last look at her art project, she stormed out of the room for lunch, convinced she would never have produced such a sculpture unless her mind had already been infiltrated by forces outside of her control. And as she hustled down the hall toward the cafeteria's deliriously cheery decor, she wondered how deep into her mind that influence might go.

CHAPTER NINETEEN

At 6:30 a.m. Sunday, Blade Northrop woke up in the back seat of his step father's cherry red Chevy Malibu, feeling like he'd been partying for days. But when? Since he started working for Yarrow, there had been zero time for fun.

"Must have *found* me some time," he mumbled through dry lips. Sitting up, he tried to focus his sticky, bleary eyes. So far, no luck. True, the sun was just coming up, but Blade kind of expected to make out shadows, at least. Maybe if he got out of the car and walked around he could get his bearings.

But as he jiggled the handle on the rear passenger side, where he must have thrown himself in the middle of the night, the door wouldn't budge. Come to think of it, wasn't the car at an angle? Better sit still and try to figure this out. With the sun steadily rising in the sky, it wouldn't be long before he had part of the answer.

Judging from the way light was pouring in, directly through the driver's side window, the car must have been tilted up toward the east. Blade's breath rasped in his throat as he realized — in spite of the glare — he still couldn't see farther than….

OK, OK, it was just his hoodie, which he'd put on backwards. Once he flipped down the fleece hood, he could see the mess he was in: The Malibu was stuck in a deep ditch in the middle of, as best he could tell, Absolutely Nowhere.

As he peered out the rear driver's side window at the road bed below, bits of the last few hours came back to him. First off, he was in deep trouble with Callie Ann. He was supposed to have met her at the movies on Sunday night.

"Totally missed that," he muttered to his car. Time for a make-up call — but what kind of excuse did he have? He'd run out of Chad stories ... OK, better get on the phone anyway. Maybe, if Callie Ann wasn't too mad….

No way, his phone was completely tapped out. That had to mean he'd been unconscious for more than 24 hours. How could he be sure? Like everything else he didn't know about the recent past, he couldn't guarantee he hadn't been talking nonstop on his phone the whole time.

Whatever. The only thing that mattered was figuring out what to do now. Mr. Yarrow must be crazy angry with him for not checking in. The first decent job of his life and here he was blowing it. And for what? A stupid party?

Except, he couldn't remember going to any party.

Taking a deep breath, Blade decided to get out and look around. Yeah, that had to be the first step. After five or six tries, he pushed the driver's-side door open. Too bad it was practically at a 45 degree angle to the ground. He'd have to climb out of the Malibu and drop down to the asphalt below.

But when he grabbed hold of the car door frame, the pain in his palms squeezed a scream out of him so fast he could barely breathe. What the freak was up with his hands? It was the fungusy stuff he'd started seeing all over his body. Right: that was half the reason he hadn't met up with Callie Ann like he was supposed to. What if he got lucky again and she took his shirt off? He had enough weird-looking patches of skin to be in a circus freak show.

But how much longer could he stay stuck out on a country road before the county sheriff drove up and started asking questions? From the way Blade's head felt, he wasn't sure he could pass a Breathalyzer test. And anyway, how would he explain how Chad Northrop's car came to be jutting out of the shoulder, jammed tight into a muddy ditch?

So, with one painful push, Blade Northrop popped himself out of his stepfather's wrecked car and landed with a rolling tuck on the muddy black top below. Yuck. Must have been raining, except way more than usual for October. Better stand up and have a look around.

Near as he could tell, he wasn't bleeding and had no broken bones. Good, for starters, but where the heck was he? Blade rubbed the back of his neck and tried to get the cricks out of his spine, but ... no, he seriously could not stand up straight.

Legs stiff, he aimed his bare feet gingerly along the slick, wet asphalt. Where were his boots?

Stopping at a green mileage sign, Blade stared at the dingy white lettering and felt his heart start working overtime:

Harmony Beach	**5**
Mt. Skye	**15**
Loganville	**35**
Skudderton	**50**

This was bad. His stepdad's car was totaled, he was covered with a weird-looking fungus, he'd probably lost his girlfriend — and he was stranded 50 miles out of town without a phone.

How did this happen? Must have been thrown off by the voices in his head. Blade had been hearing them since his first meeting with Mr. Yarrow — from the moment the intense, wiry man had grabbed his forearm.

At first, he'd mistaken the sensation for an earache, but lately.... Right, he remembered now: The voices had risen to a deafening level just past the Mt. Skye exit, making it harder and harder to concentrate on the road until....

OK, he was seriously screwed. As if that ugly stuff on his skin wasn't bad enough, now he was going insane.

Having picked his way back to the car, Blade hopped up, pulled himself into the driver's side door, squeezed into the space behind the driver's seat and rummaged around for his boots. They had to be ... There! But what was this? Oh yeah, the package he was supposed to deliver to a mailbox in Harmony Beach.

And as the sun rose higher in the sky, the exhausted boy felt his memory trickle back into place, soothing his aching mind with a reassuring sense of orientation. Yes. Mr. Yarrow, Harmony Beach, and a special mailbox right near the ocean's edge. Really weird, but, the money.... Mr. Yarrow had promised him double his usual rate if he delivered the package on time.

Trouble was, Blade had no idea what day it was. That meant his only chance of hooking up with Callie Ann again was to get over to Harmony Beach, make the delivery and hope one of Mr. Yarrow's contacts could help him out with the Malibu. Or at least give him bus fare back to Skudderton. Either way, he had to get moving.

So, much as the thought of a five-mile hike made his head swim, Blade dug a pair of ratty gym socks out of his left boot, fumbled them on with swollen fingers — then fought his boots onto his blotchy, tender feet.

Minutes later, curious drivers along Route 72 East were shaking their heads at the sight of a teenage boy clutching a muddy, gray hoodie around his lanky frame — his eyes sunken, his skin pale and blotchy, his gait an awkward, lurching shuffle.

And as he covered the five-mile stretch of narrow country roads, dodging gravel trucks, delivery vans and the menacing stares of starving stray dogs, Blade Northrop's one thought was whether he could check himself into an emergency room without giving away Mr. Yarrow's secret.

Stopping for the fifth time in half an hour to make sure the package was still stuffed snugly into his jeans, Blade's neck twitched at the thought of what he'd seen in the back room of the post office — the one place Mr. Yarrow had told him never to go.

Having stuck his head around the edge of the threshold when none of Yarrow's silent operatives was looking, Blade had seen his Team Leader talking to a huge computer screen hovering in the middle of the room. But the screen, which for all Blade knew was available at Best Buy, wasn't the weird part. It was the slimy, yellow glop of ... whatever ... on the screen — and the screeching, raspy voice Mr. Yarrow used to talk to it — that told Blade he'd stumbled on something no one on Earth had encountered before.

CHAPTER TWENTY

Lena looked across the cafeteria table at Callie Ann's red, teary eyes and felt her stomach twist. For once, that had nothing to do with the Sloppy Joe a food server had plopped down on her plate. Listening to Callie Ann's worries about Blade Northrop was stirring her own worst fears and causing the mob-scene voices in her head to flare up into a dull roar every time Callie Ann said his name.

What had happened? Or rather, what did Callie Ann think had happened? The longer Lena's best friend talked, the harder it was to keep track. Best as Lena could make out, "Blainy" had disappeared a few days ago, shortly after starting his new delivery job.

"First, he was all happy," said Callie Ann, digging her fork into the soggy hamburger bun on her plate. "Said he was going to be rich."

Then his mood had darkened and he hardly spoke, wouldn't look at her, and was constantly mumbling about "The Team."

"Last time we were together he wouldn't even let me touch him," said Callie Ann, blowing her nose into her napkin.

OK, that was gross, but Lena forced herself to not focus on Callie Ann's bad habits — the worst of which was her scruffy, chain-smoking boyfriend. What was complicated about this situation? The big jerk had obviously found an illicit way to make lots of money and had skipped town. But for Callie Ann's sake, Lena struggled to help her friend save face, reinforcing her delusion that if Blade had broken off contact, he must be trapped, hurt or unconscious.

"Don't his parents know anything?" Lena asked.

"They don't even have his cell number," sobbed Callie Ann again. "They're both so out of it, especially his stepdad."

"When was the last time you.... " Lena began.

What little Lena could make out from Callie Ann's slurred, weepy voice involved a frantic phone call late yesterday — during which Blade babbled and screamed incoherently about "the voices in my head" and "the mailbox by the ocean."

"And what the freak is a 'transmog chamber'?" asked Callie Ann. "Was he on drugs? I have no clue ... the phone just died. Then yesterday I heard ... the police ... they called Blainy's stepdad about the car. I don't even know if.... "

"Where was it?" asked Lena, reaching out her hand to Callie Ann's pretty, tear-soaked face. "The car, I mean."

"Cops found it in a ditch!" Callie Ann yelled, turning heads in her direction from across the cafeteria. Closing her eyes, Lena realized she'd better get Callie Ann out of the cafeteria before Mr. Cosentino got wind of her outburst.

Whatever Blade was up to, if it involved a crime, Callie Ann might end up being a suspect in a police investigation. At least, that's the way it worked on TV. But that was the trouble with being a kid, even an older kid. You had to make important decisions before you even had time to sort out reality from fantasy.

Not that the adults in her life seemed much better at it. Listening to Dad talk to Rhea about his plan to become a full-time cruise ship captain, Lena had to wonder if he even remembered she was planning to go to college the year after next.

"What ditch ... where?" Lena whispered, hoping Callie Ann would take the hint. But hearing the answer, Lena could barely keep from yelling, herself.

"Was there anything else, like, funny about Blade the last time you saw him?" asked Lena, standing up with her tray.

"Yeah," said Callie Ann following her lead. "He had this weird kind of blotchy stuff on his arms. I was going to ask you about it.... " she added, before choking up in tears again.

OK, that sealed it. Hearing voices, skin problems and headed for a mailbox stuck in the middle of Harmony Beach — where Lena had seen an unknown aircraft splash down in August.

As she walked Callie Ann out of the cafeteria and into the girl's locker room, Lena felt a twinge wriggle through her spine. Whatever was behind the strange events of the last month, it had started with the ship she was definitely not supposed to have seen. And the day after the splashdown, who showed up?

She had to find Derek. She had to risk everything and confront him with what she knew. Because as scared as she had been by the voices she'd heard on the his radio, she figured they had to be part of the answer.

Leaving Callie Ann with a couple of her other friends in Gym class, Lena was relieved the two of them didn't have exactly the same schedule the way they had in 8th grade. As she headed down the hall, she realized she needed time alone to think this through.

Heading for her locker on the first floor, Lena wondered if there was a connection between the appearance of Derek and the disappearance of Blade. While she was pretty sure it wasn't a coincidence, it made no sense that Derek could have anything to do with ... with murder. And yet the voices in her head and the voices on his dad's radio ... OK, they didn't sound exactly alike. But they did sound exactly as *alien.*

The thought of Derek being an extra-terrestrial made Lena's lunch lurch a little too close to her throat, but the evidence pointed in only one direction. And in that moment, she realized how hard she'd been working to deny it. Derek and his parents didn't just have different customs, like people from another country. They were disconnected, apart ... other....

"Time for an experiment," Lena whispered to the water fountain on her right. On impulse, she ducked into the girl's room, hurried into the back stall and shut the door tight. Pressing her fingers to her temples, for no particular reason, she tried to focus her mind on one thought:

Where is Derek? Derek, can you hear me?

You don't have to scream, said Derek's voice in her head, sounding way more mature than usual.

"Derek?" said Lena out-loud.

Use your mind, Derek's stern voice echoed. *You want people to think I'm in the girl's room with you?*

Sorry.... thought Lena.

Come over to my house after school, said the voice in Lena's head, sounding more like the Derek she knew. *I need some help with my parents.*

What ... are they ... what's the matter.... Lena's mind stuttered.

They're kind of dead, said Derek. *And I have you to thank for it.*

Just then the class buzzer rang out, breaking their mentallic connection and nearly knocking Lena off her feet. What a life. She'd just heard the most shocking sentence ever — and instead of having time to react, she had to rush off to Dad's History class.

As she hurried out of the girl's room and up to the third floor, she wondered if there were any greater punishment in the universe than being a teenager. No matter what was going on in her life, she always had to follow a set of dumb rules. What did Derek mean? He had her to thank for *what*? Whatever the answer, she'd have to wait — until Dad was finished filling her head with a lot of boring stuff about Andrew Jackson and the Battle of New Orleans.

CHAPTER TWENTY-ONE

Stumbling down the Brazilian hardwood steps of the deserted boardwalk at Harmony Beach, Blade Northrop fought against his pounding heart and the throng of clamoring voices in his head. Distracted by the crashing waves of the ocean on his left, he slipped on the last step and fell face down into a mound of cold, wet sand. Choking and coughing, he nearly suffocated in the unforgiving silica until he managed to pull himself up to his knees.

As he struggled to his feet, he thought he heard Mr. Yarrow's voice roaring out at him over the confused chatter echoing through his mind. The mailbox, the package, the beach, 230 yards SSW along the shoreline ... each word in Mr. Yarrow's harsh accent stabbed at Blade's brain like a straight razor.

And yet, through the fog of pain and regret that dominated his mind, Blade was relieved to know he was still part of the Team. Not that the Team had done much for him; he hadn't seen a cent of the money Mr. Yarrow promised him since the day he signed on.

And come to think of it, half of *that* money — the bills he hadn't already spent — had exploded into a weird kind of sticky powder in his shirt pocket. The next day, the painful itching began in his chest and gradually spread down both arms and legs. Until now ... now he could barely move. The swollen, itchy patches on his skin, looking like an insane mutation, made his joints throb and turned his every breath into a heavy, painful sigh. Worse, he was desperate with hunger, but the thought of food itself was totally disgusting.

"Gotta stand up for myself," he mumbled. "Get me some hardship pay or whatever."

But for now he had to focus on the mailbox, the one he was supposed to find way out here on this abandoned stretch of beach. Wait. Was that it? No, just a heap of coiled up dune fencing ... what? ... turn right....

So he continued for the next hour, his progress delayed by several falls into the wet sand, including the time he slammed down hard on a jagged shard of oyster shell. The white calcite had easily ripped through the fungoid layers in his palms and sent a trickle of blood and searing pain down each wrist. Callie Ann would never believe his cover story now. And if he tried to tell her the truth ... well forget it. Forget about Callie Ann until he reached the mailbox and ... There! That had to be it ... or maybe not.

For one thing, the cylindrical object in front of him couldn't be real.

"Looks like that postcard," Blade muttered, thinking of the photo tacked to the wall above his dresser: a street scene, with a bright red English mailbox at the center. The photo, he remembered, was on a postcard Chad Northrop had sent two years ago, soon after sleeping through his second week of bookings at a seaside resort in Brighton.

So what was *that* mailbox doing here? No way Blade could have driven the Malibu across the ocean....

Despite his doubts, the sound of Mr. Yarrow's voice in Blade's head drove him on, urging him to deposit the package he'd shoved down his jeans into a slot near the top of the object.

At last, Blade was close enough and, hands trembling, he managed to fumble the package out and deposit it in one of the slots near the top of the red cylinder. The mailbox opened out toward him like a set of double doors and the rumbling crowd sounds in his head died away, leaving only Mr. Yarrow's voice echoing in Blade's mind.

"Get in," said the voice.

"No," Blade whispered hoarsely, "No more ... orders ... until you ... you pay me."

And as the wind whipped up over the ocean, Blade was knocked over by a powerful stream of paper money, shooting out at him from the mouth of the mailbox. His breathing ragged, Blade scrambled for the bills, reaching his stiff, bleeding hands out to grab as many as he could before, once again, Mr. Yarrow's voice echoed in his mind.

"Get in," growled Yarrow, "and earn what you deserve."

Clutching huge, wet wads of 20s, 50s and 100s in each hand, Blade crawled into the waiting maw of the cheery English mailbox. Once inside, his weary ache of a head was briefly soothed by the thought of the make-up present he could now buy Callie Ann: a diamond necklace, or a set of solid gold earrings. Girls liked stuff like that and Callie Ann ... Callie Ann ... Callie....

In a blaze of light, the red cylinder slammed shut around him and winked out of view, taking Blade and a small pile of sand with it — and sending a veritable dune of paper money fluttering out to sea on a gust of icy wind.

CHAPTER TWENTY-TWO

Staring down at Derek's parents, as they lay motionless, inside a large, sleek compartment, Lena wondered why she wasn't more frightened. Maybe it was because George and Sarah Dixon didn't look so much dead as ... as switched off, each face a mask of frozen indifference.

It should have been a terrifying sight, like a scene from one of Silvano's favorite horror movies. Yet fear never entered Lena's mind. She was too busy getting grossed out by how inhuman Derek's parents looked — like two AA batteries tucked in the back of a travel alarm clock.

Good thing she'd asked Vance to tag along for a reality check. After her mentallic conversation with Derek from the girl's bathroom at school, she figured Vance's straight-shooting attitude would help her get her bearings again. Trouble was, from the look on his face, Vance wasn't holding up very well. Cursing herself, Lena realized her mistake: She'd been *expecting* something weird at Derek's house. Vance, on the other hand....

"Dude, what's this about?" asked Vance. "You telling me you electrocuted your own parents?"

Derek held up his hands for silence, then peeled back a section of DXN/GRG's forehead, exposing the iridium casing of the metadigital neural network the robot had used as a brain.

"Maybe you better start from the beginning," said Lena, taking Derek's hands in hers.

"There's no point," said Derek, turning away to open the bedroom's vertical blinds — and cast a glance at the mailboxes clumped together on the sidewalk only a few feet away. Turning back he added, "There's no point, unless you're willing to help me."

But what Derek meant by "helping" had a ring of danger about it neither Lena nor Vance was sure they were ready for.

"Check it ... those wack mailboxes are an invasion force?" asked Vance.

And though the answer was "yes," Lena soon learned the truth was even more complex — starting with the fact that Derek was an alien and — even scarier — an exiled criminal.

"But why do you have to get involved?" asked Lena. "Don't you have an army or ... or a police force where you come from?"

Derek hung his head.

"It falls to me," was all he would say.

Quieting her fears, Lena decided to help him. If she needed proof of Derek's story, it was right inside her head. These days, a rising and falling tide of mentallic chatter echoed across her mind constantly and invaded her dreams. Besides, Derek's plan was clear, even if she doubted she'd ever understand it completely.

But as much as she could see Derek's counterstrike against the Vrukaari would probably succeed in a general way, she was worried the details might keep her from doing her part. Like how in the world she would convince Dad to let her borrow the car for an off-season visit to Harmony Beach.

Derek had offered to influence Dad with a kind of mind control but, as Lena suspected, the risk of brain damage was too great. What good was saving the world — only to lose the most important person in it?

But the stakes were that high. The three of them had to get to Harmony Beach as soon as possible after they'd finished the preliminary steps. Vance saw it, too; with the evidence of the two disabled robots in front of him, he didn't need any more convincing.

And yet, Lena wondered, what if they were both being deceived? What if Derek himself was the leader of the invasion, the source of the mailboxes, the fungus and the disappearance of Blade Northrop? He was a criminal, after all. Wouldn't getting Blade out of the way leave Derek free to....

Really? echoed Derek's voice in Lena's mind.

Sorry, thought Lena. *I guess I'm scared.*

Vance looked up from the two DXN units and scowled at Lena and Derek as they stared at each other in silence.

"Yo," said Vance, clapping his hands. "Somebody in the room doesn't have the mind-reading thing going on."

"You're not missing much," said Lena, even though her mentallic connection to Derek was the most fascinating thing she'd ever experienced. Derek ... whoever this guy was ... questions were forming faster than she could ask them.

"So what do you think?" asked Derek.

"I'm thinking…. " said Vance, holding his forehead. "Maybe we could use these robots for spare parts for ... I don't even know what."

"Not those," said Derek. "They've been corrupted by the Vrukaari fungus. But there are other components on the lander."

"Lander?" asked Lena.

Rolling his eyes, Derek tried his best to explain the facts of life in the rest of the universe, which Lena and Vance were surprised to learn was a lot emptier than they expected. Derek's people alone had explored and settled hundreds of habitable planets over the last 5,000 years or so. But through the centuries they had discovered only a handful of other sentient species including, unfortunately, the Vrukaari.

"So it was the Vrukaari lander I saw?" asked Lena, struggling to piece together a new reality out of the scrambled bits of memory and startling new information that now swirled through her mind like snowflakes on the wind.

As Derek explained, the autonomous navigation system on board his Snaldrialooran lander had switched to stealth mode long before entering the atmosphere. Far from burning up in the night sky, *his* lander had slipped noiselessly through the clouds and into the ocean 20 miles south of Harmony Beach. Uncomfortably close to the Vrukaari, but at no time in danger of detection.

That was the difference, Derek noted with guilty pride, between true spacecraft and technologies slapped together from scavenged components and stolen engineering diagrams. The Vrukaari ship Lena had seen? Probably built by a team of offworld technicians, trembling at gunpoint.

Casting a worried look at his two friends, Derek wondered how he dared involve them in an intergalactic battle — with no strike force and only a sketchy tactical plan. And it didn't help any that Lena would have to squeeze saving the planet in between helping her dad get ready for his wedding in 10 days or less.

"I thought Earth weddings were planned out months in advance," he said, rubbing his neck.

"Usually," said Lena, her eyes settling on Derek's intergalactic transponder, now resting snugly on the black leather couch the DXN units had ordered from Raymour and Flanigan.

"Besides," said Vance. "You made it sound like we don't have much more time than that, anyway."

"Maybe less," said Derek. "Remember that game you were working on?"

Over the next few hours, Derek laid out his plan, a tactical strike on the Vrukaari mentallic network, combined with a stealth attack on its Earth-based command, which was headed by grim Mr. Yarrow.

"With luck," he said, "we should be able to disrupt the Vrukaari and their transmog technology in a matter of hours, once we get everything in place."

"Dude," said Vance, smacking his forehead. "If we were lucky, none of this would be happening."

And in that moment, Derek, feeling more like Ixdahan every minute, finally realized the full weight of his crime. For it was he, and he alone, who was responsible for the crisis now surrounding Vance and Lena's entire planet.

CHAPTER TWENTY-THREE

From the moment Rhea Silber arrived from Boston, Lena's life was split down the middle. While Lena-One was immersed in Rhea's plan for an improvised wedding ceremony, Lena-Two was knee deep in Derek's plan to save the planet. Then there was the whole high school thing, the snarling beast that devoured her time, slurped down her energy and roared for more.

Still worse, the voices in Lena's head were now as clear as a cell phone conversation. At first, she'd heard only a murmuring, punctuated every so often by a piercing shriek.

But since making mentallic contact with the Snaldrialooran transponder, her mind was now tuned in to military strategy sessions taking place light years from Earth. The topic? A series of tactical strikes against isolated planets near Snaldrialoor.

Sitting up on the edge of her bed, Lena wondered why she had to take on Derek's burden. Couldn't she go to the police, tell *them* about the Vrukaari, then go to the hospital — and have her brain yanked out?

She squeezed her eyes shut tight, as she remembered her last attempt to explain things to the doctors at Skudderton General. This time, she figured, they might lock her away for observation.

On the other hand, weren't the mutant mailboxes weird enough to back up her story? Breathing hard, Lena stumbled over to her laptop and reopened the YouTube video she'd seen the night before. There! The Governor's conference in Austin, Texas: 44 men and 6 women arguing over how to handle the random clumps of mailboxes now cropping up in small towns from Nobleton, Florida to White Mountain, Alaska.

Trouble was, their absence in New York, Los Angeles, Chicago, Houston, Philadelphia, Phoenix or any other major U.S. city had led many members of Congress to adopt a wait-and-see attitude, pending a "full investigation of this alleged prank."

Gazing out through her bedroom window at the faded swing set in her backyard, Lena wondered who the senators thought could pull off such a stunt. And, by the way, how come every police stakeout so far had drawn a blank?

Take the video she saw on CNN.com yesterday: Police officers stationed in their cars at night to watch the street corners in Saugatuck, Michigan were found next morning lying on the doorstep of City Hall, sound asleep in their boxer shorts — right across the street from the latest clump of mailboxes.

And though the newscast failed to mention it, Lena noticed the blotchy patches of skin on the unhappy men's legs as they trudged into waiting police vans.

"Wonder if they're hearing voices already," she mumbled.

Fortunately, there was one thing that could silence the voices in her own head: the look on Dad's face. Through the long years since Mom ... since ... Lena had never seen his face brighten the way it did now. These days, he was involved again, in more than work, in more than keeping the *Shari Lynn* shipshape through the winter.

Not that it didn't have its downside. In the last two weeks, he'd been on her case about homework, about building a portfolio for college and, incredibly, about boys.

"I'm worried about you," he'd said after dinner one night when Rhea had gone to bed early. "You never seem to, you know, go out anymore."

OK, as if this business with Derek and the Vrukaari wasn't nightmarish enough, Lena was stuck trying to explain her dating status to her dad. It was another reason she hoped Silvano would come back to the States.

Only not yet. If he knew ... if the Vrukaari would let her tell him what was going on, she was sure Silvano would want to help. Yet the thought of introducing him to Derek, well, that would be too confusing.

So, as Dad tried to pin her down, Lena decided a shard of Truth might be the best defense against parental nosiness.

"I'm kind of seeing Derek, the new boy," said Lena. "Only his parents don't let him out of the house much."

"Maybe we could invite him over to dinner this week," said her father in the Helpful Dad voice that was the one thing on Earth Lena hated more than Harvard beets. "Want me to talk to Mr. and Mrs. Dixon about it?"

"I'll work it out," said Lena, patting his hand. "They just need more time to find out how fabulous I am."

Later that afternoon, dozing off over her Advanced Bio lab book with Arkansas curled up in her lap, Lena was awakened by the sensation of Derek knocking on her brain.

Derek? she thought. *Is that you?*

You better hope so, said Derek. Funny how much steadier and confident he sounded since his "parents" were ... deactivated.

I'm not ever going to get used to this, am I? asked Lena, her heart racing in her chest.

Of course you are, said Derek. *Soon, mentallic communication will become as natural as....*

No, said Lena. *I can't get used to you being an alien.*

Think how I feel, said Derek.

But, as he pointed out, they had plenty else to get crazy about. Lena's mentallic connection with Derek meant he could show her images from the Galactic Array, even if she couldn't access them directly.

What she saw made her throat go dry.

You're kidding, right? asked Lena. *This isn't....*

But it was real. The scene of devastation at the rural village in Nova Scotia was disturbing, yet so remote that it hadn't reached the news outlets, even online.

How soon can you deliver the metal casing? asked Derek.

OK, this was going to be harder than she had realized. Though Derek knew a lot of basic facts about Earth, he didn't know much about the way things worked. Like the fact that Lena couldn't use the Metal Shop whenever she wanted.

Lucky for her, making the container would be easy. The tricky part was coming up with an explanation her teacher would buy. "Vase" wouldn't cut it.

But don't we have to test your plan first? she asked.

No time, said Derek. *Besides, I have a backup plan — I think.*

Lena flinched as Dad's voice echoed up the staircase, calling her down for dinner.

"Time to go," she whispered aloud. "I'll see if I can switch to the Monday after school class."

But.... said Derek.

"Can't you stall the bad guys with that radio thingie of yours?" asked Lena.

What do you think I've been doing? said Derek.

Closing her mind, Lena ran down the stairs, glad to trade the weirdness of mentallic conversation for the normality of dinner. Except this dinner wasn't exactly normal, either. It was one of the last meals Lena would eat before the wedding — before Dad's girlfriend was "transmogged" into Lena's stepmother. All the more reason she was grateful for one more touch of soothing comfort: lime Jell-O with homemade whipped cream for dessert.

CHAPTER TWENTY-FOUR

Deep in the ruined shell of the Skudderton post office, a quiet whir of machinery was the only sound — audible to no one but the scarred walls of what was once a typical American municipal building from the 1930s.

In a far corner, a pale blue light flickered down to reveal a shuddering figure, lying in a contraption any visitor could have easily mistaken for a misplaced tanning booth. Any visitor daring to take a closer look might have also thought the person trapped inside the booth was dying.

Yet the one visitor who did enter the deserted hulk of 78-year-old limestone, granite, glass and steel suffered from neither of these delusions.

Pushing up the loose-fitting sleeves of his blue, crushed velvet jumpsuit, he stared down at a gleaming display panel. His jaw tensed as he gazed over at the one person on Earth who would recognize him: the lanky teenage boy, now lying unconscious, in what was definitely not a tanning booth.

Status lights on the reverse-engineered transmog chamber blinked in a dizzying pattern, as the wiry, middle-aged man stared, brow furrowed, watching for the tell-tale signs of system failure.

Not that he cared a handful of interstellar gas what became of the boy in any moral sense. But at this stage in the mission, finding and reprogramming another Earth creature would count as a major setback — something his exalted superiors would never have understood.

The man ran his transmogged fingers over a touch screen, cursing its shoddy construction, as he entered a new set of commands. With equipment like this he was expected to launch a decisive invasion of a virtually unknown planet? The Panel would hear his complaints the moment he returned in victory. Trouble was, victory hinged on reviving the rebellious boy from transmog coma. There! It would either work or it wouldn't; the result was out of his hands.

As he stepped away from the whirring device, Relsheesharb Yarrow pushed back the hood of his jumpsuit and broke into a smile. Though it would be several hours before the boy was fully functional, the chamber's artificial intelligence reported that Blade Northrop's vital signs had returned to normal.

Yarrow's relief didn't last long. No sooner had he completed the main-stage restoration of the Earth creature, than the Vrukaari soldier's mind flooded with a larger problem: The unexplained mentallic static that blocked access to the sectors of the Galactic Array not already disrupted by the Interstellar Consortium.

As if those prim busybodies had any right to interfere with legitimate Vrukaari planetary colonization protocols. By his own direct experience, the Consortium's claim that those efforts impinged on the sovereignty of an existing sentient species were baseless, a pure power play.

Sentient? By now, Yarrow had studied Earth's electronic transmissions for countless hours. That they were anything other than the squawkings of a pre-literate society was ridiculous.

No doubt a crew of illegal space traders had swept this region centuries ago. They must have planted the seeds for the primitive technologies these sub-sentient creatures claimed to have invented for themselves.

More likely, the entire species had been bred like pets, taught a few tricks and then abandoned, the moment richer prey was discovered. He'd go to great pains to include these observations in his report — a report he was sure would earn him the recognition of his exalted superiors, and perhaps command of a large-scale investigation of illegal trade across the unknown sectors.

A fleeting grin disrupted Yarrow's otherwise perpetual scowl. For his new command would also earn him a seat at the table with the traders themselves, and a healthy share of their illegal profits, paid out in hush money and special favors.

Yes, he could turn this graveyard assignment to his advantage after all, if only he could set his plan in motion with no further interference from ... whatever was jamming his transmissions. But what could it be? Not the Snaldrialooran prisoner; he was being held under close robotic supervision. No, the mentallic static must be a temporary inconvenience, a technical glitch to be worked out in a matter of hours.

And yet, perhaps there was one other candidate for a terrorist assault on the Array: The young Earth female the Lander Team had so carelessly alerted to their presence. If it were up to him, she would have been killed on the spot, but his orders were countermanded. "No overt intervention before preparations are complete," read the Panel's sealed invasion protocols. As if any set of rules weren't made to be ignored when the time came.

Could the careless use of a neuro-receptor fungus have altered her brain functions? Would it have been sufficient to endow such a low-level consciousness with the ability to access the Galactic Array? Or had these savages amassed enough medical knowledge to reprogram the fungus for their own purposes as part of their "cure?"

Nonsense.

Snorting, the Vrukaari officer realized how little it mattered. Looking down at the pathetic boy who was slowly reaching full consciousness, Lieutenant Colonel Yarrow knew he had the tools in place to deal with the girl, should she, as was highly unlikely, pose a threat to the Plan.

By sheer luck, this boy had a social connection to the girl — while the girl herself, as his own scan of her mind had told him, had a singular vulnerability he could exploit with ease. That is, except for the subtle way the fungus had reordered her brainwave patterns, making it hard to scan her mind or interpret it with absolute clarity. And that, he decided, made her continued presence in his vicinity an unacceptable liability. If there were any chance she was connected to the Snaldrialooran or was otherwise not altogether what she seemed, "Lena Gabrilowicz" would have to be eliminated at once.

Satisfied with his analysis, the battle-scarred soldier chuckled at the sight of the blinking "ready" light on the transmog chamber. Releasing the catches on the containment dome, he stood back and waited as the shivering, naked Earth boy propped himself up on one elbow. For his part, Blade Northrop was more perplexed by the grin on his master's face than by anything else that had happened in the last 72 hours.

CHAPTER TWENTY-FIVE

Standing in Derek's living room, Vance fought hard to accept the way Reality kept shifting gears.

"You're serious, aren't you?" asked Vance, squinting. "We're going to, like, beam over to your ship?"

Derek counted to eight.

"If it helps you to think about quantum transfer technology in terms of your televised mythology," he said, "go ahead. I don't have the time or the expertise to explain it. But it's at least as safe as your internal combustion vehicles."

"You mean *cars*?" snapped Vance. "Could you talk like a normal guy, for once?"

"You want to rethink that question?" asked the alien, pulling an ominous black disk off a low lying shelf in the hall linen closet.

"Forget it," said Vance. "Just try not to sound like a ... like the freakin' Duke of New Jersey," he added. "How'd you get to be so damn *serious* all of a sudden?"

"The DXN units were equipped with cortical dampeners," Derek began, "designed to inhibit.... "

"OK, OK," said Vance, pushing his glasses back onto the bridge of his nose. "It's like you said: Complicated. I just wish I.... " he added, staring at the disk. "What the McNuggets is that thing?"

As Derek fussed with the settings on a small console he'd popped out of the disk, he tried his best to explain the theory of quantum signature reassignment — with only partial success.

Essentially, the disk, which seemed to have doubled in size since Derek set it down on the coffee table, wouldn't *take* them to the Snaldrialooran lander. It would rewrite their space-time coordinates so they'd *be* in the lander.

"I guess it's no use asking you if that's even possible," said Vance, feeling like an idiot. "But what if something goes wrong and...."

"And we rematerialize inside a tree?" asked Derek. "In the first place, we won't be dematerializing. If we did, there wouldn't be any 'us' left to rematerialize, unless you see yourself as a lifeless lump of biochemical components."

"So, no tree?" asked Vance, wringing his hands.

"No," said Derek, as he flipped a toggle switch on the disk and, a nanosecond later, looked up to survey the interior of the Snaldrialooran lander that had brought him to Earth six weeks earlier. "At least, it's pretty unlikely," he added.

"Whoa!" said Vance, craning his neck and torso to take in this startling change of scenery. "Give a dude a little warning?"

Derek reached up to put his hands on Vance's shoulders.

"Try to stay calm," he said. "From here on out you're going to see a lot of things you're not used to. But I can't do this without you, and if I fail ... well, you don't want to be ruled by the Vrukaari."

"What are they, like, tyrants?" asked Vance, leaning in.

"More like complete, bungling idiots," said Derek, "but with a nasty streak."

"OK," said Vance. "Why are we here?"

"Looking for enough spare parts to patch a solution together," Derek said at last. "Starting with that programming module over there."

Vance looked where Derek was pointing and shook his head.

"That boxy thing?" he asked. "How am I gonna program with that?"

"It's already configured for human interface," said Derek. "How do you think my humanoid robots used it?"

"Magic wand?" asked Vance, rolling his eyes.

As they continued to collect supplies, which Derek stacked on a floating platform that followed him everywhere, Vance struggled with explanations he knew he would have to accept as the truth. It didn't make any less sense than the picture Derek had shown him hours before — of the eight-tentacled, liquid methane-breathing creature Derek had identified as "me."

"So, you download everything you need to know from a ... from, like, a galactic Web site?" asked Vance, tiptoeing behind the transmogged Snaldrialooran.

"Not everything," said Derek. "I learned how to be scared out of my mind the hard way."

Minutes later, Derek entered a series of commands into a small access panel, sending the two of them and the floating platform back to his living room.

"Can't get used to that," said Vance, leaning over to help Derek unload their alien cargo.

"And I can't get used to having legs," said Derek. "Yet somehow, I've got to save an entire species of sentient, bipedal gas breathers."

"Great," said Vance. "Now you're making me feel like an alien."

"Kind of stings, doesn't it?" said Derek, turning away to unload the platform.

"So ... how exactly can I help you with this?" asked Vance. "You gonna sell the Vru ... Vrukaari a video game?"

"No," said Derek, "they're not going to play a game. They're going to get played by it."

"Think you're pretty smart, don't you?" said Vance, smacking his forehead. "Except I have no idea what you.... "

"We'll transmit the gaming software right into their sensors," said Derek, "and let them see the vision of Earth we want them to see."

"So they'll think my SIM Google Earth is the real thing?" said Vance. "Sweet. But can't you just, you know, with your mind.... "

"Sure, for an hour, maybe," said Derek, rubbing his temples.

"Too bad," said Vance, "'cause I don't know how I'm gonna...."

"One thing at a time," said Derek, turning toward the floating platform. "Help me unload this equipment."

CHAPTER TWENTY-SIX

Callie Ann scuffed her sneakers along the shoreline, pausing only to look out over Felicity Bay for signs of ... anything ... that might give her clues. What had happened to Blainy? The car the police towed out of the ditch five miles away had nothing unusual in it: no drugs or alcohol — and no suicide note.

It was like Blainy had stopped driving altogether, like he'd fallen asleep at the wheel and veered off to the right. Good thing there were few highway lights standing along these country roads and, by luck, he'd missed a telephone pole only a few yards back.

So what did happen? It made no sense. Worse, in the cafeteria yesterday, she'd caught a clear vibe from Lena that Blade must be hiding out until he thought it was safe to resurface.

But Lena hadn't heard Blainy on the phone. No way he had any master plan that night; he'd sounded totally crazy.

Stopping again to stare at the waves in the cold autumn air, Callie Ann wished she could dive in and lose herself under the surface.

"Should have brought my wetsuit," she mumbled, lingering at the edge of the sand. Not that even a head-clearing swim could have washed the confusion away. What was Lena so upset about when she called this morning?

In the cafeteria, Lena had been the one trying to calm Callie Ann down. Now Lena was the one talking in freakin' circles — about needing Callie Ann to come over "right away."

Too bad. By the time Lena called, Callie Ann had already headed out for Harmony Beach in the dinged-up silver Corolla her dad had bought for her 17th birthday. Kicking the sand with her Vivid Pink Nikes, she tried to put the pieces together. What could make Lena so crazy worried?

Callie Ann stooped down to pick up a stick that had washed up on shore and stabbed at the sand, letting her mind wander the same way she had when she was little. Only now, instead of exploring the world, her only thought was finding a way to escape from it. Maybe drawing a smiley face, like she used to, would cheer her up, take her mind off....

Wait, was that her cell?

"Blainy?" she breathed into the glossy white iPhone 4 she took everywhere. He was alive! But while the voice in her ear sounded familiar, its cheery, positive tone was distant, objective — as if her scruffy, misfit boyfriend had morphed into a fun-loving counselor at a Lutheran day camp. As glad as she was to hear from him, what he was saying sounded kind of insane.

"What are you smoking?" she asked. "You disappear for a week without calling and expect me to drop everything?"

"Listen," said Blade, lowering his voice, "a lot of things are about to change. I only want to keep you safe."

"Safe from what?" asked Callie Ann, as she continued poking through the sand with her stick. What was that shiny thing buried down there?

"Just be ready," said Blade, sounding breezy and bland again. "I'll take you some place nice."

But before she could answer, Callie Ann's ears filled with the sound of a commotion in the background. "Where the heck are you?" she yelled.

"Gotta go," said a voice she didn't recognize — and the line went dead. Her first thought was to hit redial, but she guessed Blade wouldn't be answering — or be able to answer — for a while. What kind of thugs was he working for? Fists clenched, she continued to poke the sand at her feet with the stick, revealing more and more of the shiny metal ... whatever it was ... buried right beneath her feet.

Having slipped her phone back into her jacket, Callie Ann dropped the stick, dropped to her knees and began clawing through the sand, gradually revealing what looked like a vast stainless steel-and-glass container. Was there anything inside? As she dug out more of the structure, she was surprised to see its curved, sloping contours stretching farther and farther into the sand.

"Too big for a coffin," she whispered.

Looking up, Callie Ann was relieved to see she was the only one on the beach at the moment. For though she couldn't turn off her curiosity, she had the vague sense she might be breaking the law. And yet, if there was no one around, why did she keep hearing voices? Had to be the surf and the sea gulls, right? That is, except that she'd lived near the shore her entire life and had never heard....

"What?" she whispered again. "Hang on a second...."

Throwing herself down onto the sand, Callie Ann cupped her hands and peered through the glass at the pulsing, flickering glob of ... who knows what ... that lay at the center of a vast underground chamber. Even at that, it was tough to see much, as the warmth of her hands kept steaming up the icy surface.

Brushing away a bit more of the sand, she turned her head, peered to the left and saw that the glowing glob was being sprayed from all sides with a disgusting, blue slime. Shivering, she jumped up and shoved her hands into the sand, which was several degrees warmer than the chamber beneath her.

But what was she thinking? She had to get photos of this to show ... somebody ... maybe Lena. Lena, she knew, would believe her or, at least, try to. And no way Callie Ann could tell any adults about this without a friend to back her up.

So, with chilly ocean breezes making her fingers go numb, she snapped as many shots as she could think of, including a few with the camera pressed tight against the glass. From time to time she stopped long enough to clear away more sand — anything to show Lena how enormous the glass and metal underground chamber must be.

Just as she finished taking her 20th shot of the exterior, her iPhone rang out again, a text message from Lena flashing on to its smudgy touch screen.

> where r u? need 2
> talk now! btw watch
> out 4 blade! :-(

"What's she know about Blainy that I don't?" wondered Callie Ann, but before she could finish her thought, a burst of pale blue light emerged from the glass chamber, sending a blast of shrieking, high-frequency sound in her direction. Nearly toppling over, she clasped her hands over her ears and ran as fast as she could, away from the shoreline. It was as if the faint sounds she'd heard a moment ago had been amplified a thousand times, until the vibrations felt as if they would cut a hole in her skull.

Inches from her car, she fumbled for her keys, leapt into the driver's seat, slammed the door tight and sat for a moment in the blessed silence. But her relief didn't last long; she still had no idea what had happened to her Blainy. Blinking away tears, she revved up her engine and spun out of the empty beach parking lot, only seconds before a state trooper would pull in as the last leg of his morning rounds. Good thing, too, Callie Ann thought. She couldn't imagine how to explain what she'd seen on the beach only a moment before.

But more important, she didn't want to delay getting back to Skudderton and finding Lena. Not only was she worried about Blade but, as she drove onto the highway, Callie Ann realized what that globby thing had reminded her of: The ugly, patchy scales she'd seen on Lena's hands the day she met Derek Dixon at Harmony Beach. Come to think of it, lots of weird stuff had happened ever since that guy turned up. And the way he looked at her ... Better not think about it, if she didn't want to end up in a ditch like Blainy.

CHAPTER TWENTY-SEVEN

Lena felt terrible about lying to Ms. Dover, her Metal Shop teacher, but at least the lie was based on truth. Rhea *had* asked Lena to go shopping after school on Tuesday — something she'd never have done if she'd given a thought to Lena's after school activity schedule. As it turned out, convincing Ms. Dover to let Lena switch classes was much easier than expected.

"That's fine, Dear," Ms. Dover had said, with a glint in her deep blue eyes. "Just don't let your boyfriend distract you too much while you're helping with the wedding."

OK, that was just rude, but Lena decided she didn't have the luxury of getting indignant. With seven billion people depending on her, it was enough that she now had a chance to complete her part of Derek's plan a day earlier. Still, the idea of her 32-year-old teacher looking at her so worldly-wise was hard to take.

"As if," she muttered on her way to her workbench. At this point, a little boyfriend trouble would be a step up from ... Crap! Had she forgotten to bring the sketch? No ... there it was, in her jeans pocket. Now she had to figure out the best way to make the small steel box Derek had sketched out for her with his surprisingly shaky hands. It was like he'd never held a pen before coming to Earth. Then again, he probably hadn't.

"Chill," she whispered, as she slid the goggles over her face. "Have to get this right the first time."

That's my beautiful girl, said a voice in her head, a voice that sounded like ... no, it couldn't be. It was the stress of the last few days ... or maybe static from the mailboxes that had clumped up just outside the Metal Shop windows. Whatever, Lena realized she had to concentrate. How much longer before Yarrow broke through Derek's defenses and….

Lena froze at the sound of heavy leather heels clomping up behind her.

Two fingers jabbed her left shoulder. Startled, she grabbed the valve on her acetylene tank, slammed it shut — and spun around to face a guy who could have been Blade's double.

Except *this* Blade Northrop looked like he might have had a shower recently.

"You seen Callie Ann?" asked Blade, his eyes as blank as marbles. "I'm getting kinda worried about her."

Lena held her breath, fighting the urge to scream. It was like one of Silvano's horror flicks coming true. Except she'd never seen a movie zombie wearing such expensive new clothes.

"Haven't seen you around for a while either," said Lena, looking around to catch Ms. Dover's eye. "Don't you have a job now?"

"I'm ... on my break," said Blade, as if listening for the answer through headphones. "If you see Callie Ann, tell her it's important," he added, his voice trembling.

"Sure," said Lena, finally making eye contact with her teacher.

"Young man, I'll have to ask you to leave," boomed Ms. Dover from across the room. "Lena's in class now."

But if Blade heard her, it didn't show on his face, a face scrubbed so clean you'd have thought he was born yesterday. A shiver ran down Lena's spine as she watched the reanimated boy scuff his shiny new cowboy boots out of Metal Shop and down the hallway to the right. Shrugging her shoulders at Ms. Dover, Lena sat back down at her workbench and, after a deep breath, settled in to work on Derek's box. She had to finish in time!

I like the way you're setting goals for yourself, said the voice in her head, this time sounding so much like Mom it was terrifying. But Lena stayed calm, figuring the hallucination must be related to the reappearance of Blade.

Though she was tempted to contact Derek, Lena decided against it. For one thing, she was afraid she'd become too distracted to work. For another, with Blade so close by, who know how easily her mentallic transmission might have been intercepted?

Willing herself to focus, Lena managed to finish welding together the steel box Derek needed. The hardest part was the cap that had to fit over one end, so her alien friend could slip in the transmitter he was building with Vance and close it tight with "molecular sealant," as Derek called it. Harder still was staying on task; the urge to give in to the illusion and have a nice long talk with a woman who sounded exactly like Mom — was almost irresistible.

Well, not exactly, and that's what saved Lena. For though the voice's tone was right, its speech-rhythms weren't. In fact, the more Lena thought about it, the more this new voice in her head reminded her of Sarah Dixon.

But despite saying "It's not real" over and over again under her breath as she raced out of Metal Shop with Derek's box tucked deep in her backpack, she couldn't stop her pounding heart from believing the hallucination's lies. Mom was alive!

Half blinded with tears, Lena ran out in to the school parking lot, where only the powerful grip of a large hand on her upper arm kept her from getting smacked in the guts by Coach Robert's Ford Explorer.

"Are you freakin' crazy?" shouted Vance, still holding tight to her arm. "What's up with you?"

Lena shook herself free, wiped her eyes on the sleeve of her jeans jacket and stared up at Vance's face, marveling at the strength and courage she could now read in his mind.

"I thought.... " she gasped, "thought I heard my mother talking to me."

"But you know it's only those Vrukaari messing with your head!" said Vance, throwing up his hands.

"Could you keep it down?" asked Lena, heading out of the parking lot and up to the city bus stop at the corner.

"Not like anybody would understand," said Vance, trudging behind.

"You're forgetting ... those," she said, jabbing a thumb in the direction of the two mailbox clusters on this street alone.

Looking around him, Vance shrugged and clapped a hand over his mouth, wiggling his eyebrows until Lena couldn't stop herself from giggling.

"Cut it out," said Lena, gasping. To keep from laughing, she turned her head away, in time to catch a glimpse of Gary Reynolds, fussing over the engine of a rusted-out Honda CB-1000-F motorcycle. "Think he knows anything?" she asked Vance. "He hangs out with Blade a lot."

"Know anything ... Gary ... No, can't see it," said Vance, stroking his chin. Lena smacked him in the chest with the palms of her hands.

"Be serious," she snapped, turning toward the other side of the parking lot where Gary sat fastening his helmet on. "I'm going to ask him."

Ignoring the scowl on Gary's face, she put on her brightest smile and strutted over to the one boy in Skudderton that Blade Northrop seemed to count as a friend.

"Callie Ann?" snarled Gary. "What am I, her mother?" Ignoring Lena's protests, he rubbed the back of his neck with one hand and added, "Might have known you didn't want to talk about me. Well guess what, I haven't seen that douche bag Blade either, so you can stop pretending to be my friend and go back to that weird new kid you like so much."

And before Lena could open her mouth, Gary had revved up the engine on his battered Honda and pulled out of the school lot with a roar. Lena stared after him, shaking her head until she felt Vance's big hand shaking her shoulders.

"Come on," he said. "Stop worrying. Callie Ann's pretty tough on her own. Whatever's going on, she can handle it."

"Why?" asked Lena. "Who do you think she is? Cat Woman?" she added, her eyes red with tears. "There's the bus. Let's go."

Seconds later, they were being jostled by the less than perfect suspension system of the city bus.

"Heading over to Derek's?" asked Vance at the next stop light. "What?" he added, watching Lena's face.

"I was hoping to hear from Callie Ann by now." said Lena. "I texted her hours ago."

"She's probably hanging out with that Blade guy," said Vance, peering out the window at two 9-year-old boys climbing on top of a cluster of mailboxes while their mothers screamed at them to get down. "Heard he showed up at school today, acting weird."

But, as Lena explained, Blade didn't know where Callie Ann was either.

"So how's your ... Science project ... going?" she asked, nudging him in the ribs with her elbow.

And as the bus rounded the corner to take them towards Derek's neighborhood, Vance looked at her out of the corner of one eye and shook his head.

"Impossible," said Vance. "You got to talk to that dude, explain a few things."

"Like what?" asked Lena, as the bus pulled up at their stop.

"Like my name isn't Steven freakin' Hawking," said Vance, holding out his hand to help her down to the street.

"Don't think he expects that," said Lena. "He only needs us to follow instructions."

"That's what's got me worried," said Vance. "I mean, do you trust this guy?"

"A lot more than I trust those mailboxes or that ... that voice," said Lena.

"You really think…. " Vance began.

"I do," said Lena, "and we better get moving," she added, hustling down the sidewalk toward Derek's spacious two-story house.

Letting themselves into Derek's living room, Lena shrieked — at the sight of Derek sprawled out face-down on the navy blue, deep pile carpet.

CHAPTER TWENTY-EIGHT

As she pulled into the Skudderton High parking lot, Callie Ann craned her neck to find a secluded spot where her car could go unnoticed. Technically, students with cars were banned from the parking lot, as a check against the kind of extracurricular activities the School Board dreaded most.

Technically, students parked there all the time.

You just had to keep from flaunting the fact that you were flouting the rules. And this afternoon, in the middle of October, when Principal Cosentino had resigned himself to another year of budget cuts, whiny teachers and a growing attendance problem, the parking lot was the farthest thing from his mind.

Not that Callie Ann was playing the odds that fine. The only thing on her mind was finding Lena and connecting with Blade. Insane phone call or no, Blade was still Callie Ann's boyfriend; she couldn't give up until she knew what his deal was. It didn't matter what Lena said. She, Callie Ann, Captain of the State Champion Varsity Swim Team, was going to decide for herself.

Too bad she already had a sinking feeling what her decision would be. If only Blade hadn't sounded so weird, she might not lose hope. But the more she thought about it, the more Blade's problems seemed way too heavy for her to handle on her own.

That's why she had to find Lena. Maybe her best friend's steady ways would help give Callie Ann's swirling thoughts more focus. Except, where was Lena?

That was the trouble with boyfriends: They made you lose track of the people you cared about most — and that made no sense. Because, Callie Ann figured, she was more likely to be talking to Lena in five years than Blade.

The thought made her heart ache. Did she really believe Blade was gone?

Slipping into the building through the side maintenance door that Mr. Yeager always left open, she avoided the obnoxious stares of the security guards and Principal Cosentino's snippy receptionist. Before long, she made her way to the student lounge off the lockers, where she hoped to catch up on the kind of gossip that might give her a clue to Blade's whereabouts.

But the only one in the lounge at the moment was grubby Gary Reynolds, holding an ice pack over one elbow, while Mrs. Upton, the School Nurse, ran to get her coat.

"Yo, what's up with the arm?" asked Callie Ann. "Land funny sneaking through the girl's locker room window?"

"Always wondered what you fantasize about," said Gary. "But you're wrong. I got this bum elbow when your crazy-ass boyfriend dragged me off my bike."

Skeptical at first, Callie Ann's heart started pounding at the story Gary told about a deranged Blade Northrop demanding to know where she was.

"Told him I didn't know anything," said Gary, sulking. "Like you'd ever even look at me long enough for me to know where you are."

Maybe if you changed your shirt more than once a week, thought Callie Ann. But realizing Gary might turn out to be her only lead, she decided she'd better dial herself down. "Did he seem ... different to you at all?" she asked.

The news was not good. For one thing, Blade was walking around as if he were blind. That is, he could see, but not so you'd notice.

"Like a zombie," said Gary, "but that's crazy, right?"

"Right," said Callie Ann, wondering how sure she could be, based on the digital photos she'd taken at Harmony Beach. Even if zombies were impossible, she was starting to think something 100 times worse might not be.

"But why'd he think you'd know where I was?" Callie Ann asked, cringing as Mrs. Upton returned with her coat.

"Saw me talking to Lena ... OW!" said Gary, as he stood up to go.

"So ... where's Lena now?" Callie Ann called after him as Mrs. Upton led him out to her car.

"Dunno. Heard her talking to Vance about that ass-face Derek," said Gary over his shoulder, earning him a scowl from Mrs. Upton as she hustled him down the hall.

"Now what?" muttered Callie Ann to the battered soda machine against the far wall. Looked like her only option was to drive over to Derek's and see if Lena was there. If he was alone and he tried anything....

"Right. Like the new kid's a player," she whispered.

Sneaking back to the maintenance entrance, Callie Ann wondered what had happened to Derek to make him such a spaz. Funny thing was, Lena liked him — and the fact that Gary Reynolds didn't was a point in Derek's favor. As she looked out over the parking lot, she saw Gary lumbering into Mrs. Upton's pale green Ford Focus — and for the first time in hours, felt the tension drain from her body.

But no sooner had her Nikes hit the asphalt than her anxiety returned — for there was Blade pacing near the passenger side of her car. Having ducked back behind a school minivan, she peeked out at what was left of the Blainy she had known: Not much. In his place was a distant stare, beaming out from Blade's body like a lighthouse beacon.

Not yet willing to confront him, Callie Ann slipped back into school and ran out of the front door, in time to run up to the corner and catch the cross-town bus; the one that would bring her closer to Derek's house and, she hoped, the only person she believed she could still trust.

CHAPTER TWENTY-NINE

Staring down at Derek's lifeless body sprawled out on the carpet, Lena felt a headache throbbing at her temples and wondered if she could trust her eyes.

"What should we do?" she asked, tugging at her hair with both hands.

"Cool it," said Vance, "maybe it's an alien pod thing, you know?"

"No, I don't!" shouted Lena. "He looks like he's.... "

"Can't you just ... that mind-reading trick...?" asked Vance, crouching down for a closer look.

Lena squeezed her eyes shut, took a deep breath and opened her mind the way Derek had taught her — so she could search for his "mentallic aura."

You in there? she asked telepathically, staring at the back of Derek's head.

Can't move, said a faint murmur in Lena's mind.

"What is it? How can we...." Lena sputtered, trying to remember everything Derek had told her about mentallic communication. She was supposed to open her mind and let the ideas flow. But words ... she needed words to hold on to.

Transponder, said Derek, his thoughts reaching Lena as if from a great distance.

"What?" said Lena, aloud.

"You got something?" said Vance, but Lena waved him away.

My Dad's radio, Derek's thoughts echoed. *Push button.*

Lena rushed over to the Snaldrialooran transponder that had given her a first encounter with another galaxy — and scared her half to death.

Which button? thought Lena, desperate to remember what Derek had done when he'd first shown her the device.

Push! Derek whispered, as if he'd used his last drop of energy to emphasize his demand.

Fearing the worst, Lena stabbed at the buttons lining the top of the transponder, eyes streaming with tears.

"It has to work," she shrieked, "it has to.... "

"What?" shouted Vance, rushing over to her. "He told you to smash that thing? Let me do it!"

"No!" Lena shouted, pushing him away.

Turn knob, said the voice in Lena's head. Did it sound stronger?

And gradually, the more she fiddled with the dials and buttons, the stronger Derek's thoughts became until....

"He's moving," said Vance, reaching down to lift Derek up by the shoulders.

"What should I.... " Lena blurted, no longer able to sustain her mentallic link with Derek.

"Just leave it on, for now," said Derek, his voice shaky, as he pushed himself up to a half-sitting position with his hands.

"What happened?" asked Vance, pulling his glasses off to wipe his eyes.

"Caught a burst of mentallic energy from the ... the Galactic Array," said Derek. "Can you help me up?"

"It was Them, wasn't it?" asked Lena, hurrying over to help Vance drag the exhausted alien to the couch.

"One specific Them," said Derek. Over the next few minutes, as Vance rummaged through the kitchen to get Derek a snack, the transmogged alien told Lena everything he'd learned about the fierce Mr. Yarrow.

"So, this Yarrow dude," said Vance, returning with a platter of three over-stuffed sandwiches, "is he, like, a general?"

"He's trouble," said Derek. "I wasn't expecting him to make a move so soon."

"Is he the reason you blacked out?" asked Lena, allowing herself the luxury of breathing again.

Not directly, as Derek explained. The kind of mental surge powerful enough to sever his connection with the Galactic Array and knock him unconscious would have to have come from a *kalthruth* — a peculiarly Vrukaari kind of power station. What Derek didn't tell Lena and Vance was how disturbing that realization was to him.

If the Vrukaari were far enough along in their invasion plan to have finished construction on a *kalthruth,* they were only days away from initiating the mass release of soldiers from the transmogged incubation chambers they'd placed around the world. What Derek also didn't want to share with his friends was that each of the thousands of mutant mailboxes now dotting the globe contained not one but a battalion of soldiers, their incubation needing only one final blast of energy to allow them to emerge fully formed.

Were the Vrukaari foolish enough to proceed directly from transmog to activation? Yes, snorted Derek, so totally yes.

"So, OK, change of plan," said Vance, shrugging. "Instead of attacking the lander we attack the kal ... the power station. Does it matter?"

"It would help," said Derek, biting into a ham and Swiss from Vance's tray, "if we knew where the *kalthruth* was. Could be anywhere."

"Can't you ... you know ... find it with a scanner or, like, a sensor?" asked Vance.

"Not without them tracing the signal back to me," said Derek, his mouth stuffed with cheese. "Besides, equipment like that would be heavily shielded — even if I did have a clue how to…. "

The squeal of airbrakes and a bus engine belching right outside Derek's house made three heads turn toward the big bay windows at the front. Seconds later, the doorbell rang, a sound Derek hadn't heard since his lunch date with Lena.

"Who the ... who's there?" asked Vance.

Lena tiptoed up to the doorway and parted the ugly lace curtains Sarah Dixon had picked out with such glee the day Derek and his DXN units had q-transferred over from the Snaldrialooran lander.

"Oh my God, she saw me," said Lena.

Callie Ann nearly knocked Lena down as she pushed open the door and was now standing in the living room with the three conspirators.

"I don't know what's going on," she shouted, her eyes filling up with tears, "but it's kinda weird. And you, you jerk," she add, shoving a fist under Derek's chin, "if I find out you did anything to hurt Blainy…. "

"Calm down," said Lena, taking Callie Ann's tight fist into her two hands and automatically sensing her thoughts. She felt traces of Derek's mind there too, soothing Callie Ann's emotions, loosening the grip of her anger.

Not that Lena blamed him. Callie Ann was a hurricane when she wanted to be and the winds were only starting to gust up.

"Why are you here?" asked Lena, forcing her face between Callie Ann's and Derek's.

And at that, Lena's beautiful, impetuous and powerfully athletic friend broke down into the sobs of a three-year-old.

"It's this," she said, holding out her iPhone to Lena. "I was looking for ... for Blainy ... at Harmony Beach, and I found this huge, ugly metal thing with windows on it under the sand."

Lena flipped through the photos Callie Ann had taken of the alien structure buried in the sand, carefully transmitting each to Derek mentallically.

"What is that?" asked Callie Ann, flopping down on the couch. "What did it do to Blainy? I saw him. He looks like ... like a ghost or a freak or ... I don't know what."

Taking a deep breath, Vance studied the look on Lena and Derek's faces.

"You're doing the mind thing again, aren't you?" he said to Lena. "Come on, clue a guy in, OK? What are you looking at?"

"*Kalthruth*," whispered Derek, his face gone pale, his eyes looking ancient and sad.

"You know what this thing is?" asked Callie Ann, her hands balling up into fists. "How could you know...."

"Never mind," snapped Derek, jumping to his feet. "How long can you hold your breath?"

CHAPTER THIRTY

Later that afternoon, as the sun was setting and most Skudderton families were sitting down to dinner, Lena trudged from the city bus stop to the outer edges of her neighborhood.

At 17, she felt 1,000 years old. Even though her brain reminded her over and over how absurd that was, Lena's heart refused to listen; her heart was on a journey of its own even imminent danger couldn't deflect.

Case in point: After a three-hour planning session at Derek's, the one thought dominating her mind was an idealized image of Dad and Rhea standing under the *chuppah* at the synagogue on Sunset Road. How sweet — and how eerie, set against the background of Vrukaari warriors drooling for conquest.

Yet as her heavy feet turned up the gravel drive to her house, Lena's heart wandered off again. As she paused before the sturdy Colorado blue spruce in her front lawn, memories of Mom seemed to stop time. Her mind flooded with the image of Mom peering at its prickly branches through the kitchen window, night after night.

"Todd! That stupid spruce keeps needling me about the dishes," Mom would call out — before tying an apron around Dad's waist and handing him the sponge.

Trouble was, time had an annoying way of rushing past, whether Lena wanted it to or not. Soon Arkansas came trotting up, rubbed his furry face on Lena's ankles and brought her heart back home to the here and now.

"You know something I don't?" she said, reaching down to scratch his ears before heading inside.

Though Lena had hoped a quiet dinner at home would soothe her nerves, the second the disappointing meal of pot roast, canned peas and instant mashed potatoes was over, Rhea dragged her out to Skudderton-Thornberry Mall. In a fit of pre-wedding hysteria, Rhea was having a major panic attack about napkin rings. Specifically, the napkin rings she'd forgotten to buy the last 27 times she'd raced over to the mall since Sunday.

"Please?" she'd asked Lena. "I can't trust my judgment anymore and you're so smart about stuff like this."

"Can't Dad...?" Lena had started, but the look in Rhea's eyes confirmed what she already knew. Taking Dad shopping was like carrying a carton of eggs on your head.

Sure, it could be done but ... honestly? The potential mess was not worth the risk. Besides, Rhea pointed out, tonight was Dad's last poker Wednesday for a long time to come.

"He comes back smelling like the inside of a furnace," said Rhea, referring, Lena hoped, to cigar smoke and beer. Not that it mattered. Whatever Rhea had meant, it was way too much information.

Sitting next to Rhea in the Touareg, Lena found the gentle bounce of the car on Black Horse Pike was lulling her into a light sleep. Only Rhea's non-stop gabbing kept Lena from drifting off completely. Forcing herself to sit up straight, she tried to wrap her mind around the dangers she faced. What if Derek needed her help with the plan and was trying to contact her by "mindphone"?

So as the Touareg rounded the corner at the Skudderton-Thornberry Mall, Lena gave herself the mental slap Derek had taught her to use whenever she needed a pull her thoughts together. For the moment, she decided to ignore the low-level buzzing that zoomed in and out of her ears every few seconds. What could it be? It was too early in the fall for the flies to come out.

"Pewter or ceramic?" she heard herself asking Rhea as they scuffed their sneakers across the parking lot.

Inside Exporter's Cove, Lena's jaw dropped at the sea of cheerful merchandise spread out before her in aisle after aisle. Seeing it now through Derek's eyes, as a member of a vast intergalactic community, the store looked unbearably primitive. "*Glargcrialdrath arglern draultur,*" she muttered to no one in particular — not realizing she'd slipped into a language thousands of years older than humanity's earliest memory.

Lucky for her, Rhea paid no attention, fixated as she was on the table cloths in Aisle Eight.

"Let's split up," Dad's fiancée suggested, running a shaky hand through her tight, blond curls. The tablecloths were proving too tempting, but the napkin ring issue had to be resolved immediately —

before the mall closed up at nine. And no sooner had Lena turned away from Rhea and toward the direction of the napkin rings than the buzzing in her ears returned, now more insistent than before.

For the moment, Lena was much more disturbed by the way Rhea was acting to give the buzzing much thought. Though Lena had only known her a short time, Rhea's fascination with housewares was so totally out of character, it was scary.

Who was tampering with her mind?

Looking back at Rhea, hovering over the tablecloth display, ogling each and every sample with a weird, sensual leer, Lena shuddered. Only one other person she knew of besides Derek, or herself in a limited way, could have entered Rhea's mind. It had to be Yarrow, the Vrukaari Lieutenant Colonel Derek had warned her about.

OK, she didn't know as much about mentallic communication as Derek, but maybe if she looked inside Rhea's mind she might be able to find the "off switch" for whatever was making her future stepmother so crazy.

"No, Dummy," she muttered, as she arrived at the napkin rings display. No sense tipping Yarrow off. If he was so unsure of her mental powers as to set a trap for her in Rhea's mind, the longer she could keep him in the dark the better.

Besides, Lena realized, one look inside her own mind and the Vrukaari soldier might ferret out the few details she'd absorbed about Derek's plan. For the moment, Yarrow might still assume Derek was too much under the influence of the DXN units to pose a threat. It was a slim hope, maybe, but Lena couldn't afford to toss it away.

"Find anything yet?" asked Rhea, as she bounced over to where Lena was standing.

"How about these…. " Lena started to say, only to watch Rhea bounce away again, this time to check out the glassware.

Helpless, Lena looked around the store, hoping to find any excuse to get Rhea back into the Touareg and go home. That's when she saw a woman at the far end of the aisle who could have been Mom, if Mom weren't….

OK, OK, settle down, she told herself. This was either a coincidence or Yarrow taking his chances. No matter what the woman was — a hallucination, a robot or a transmogged schnauzer from the local kennel — it couldn't be Mom waving to her in the distance. That is, even if she did tilt her head at the right angle and smile the crooked smile Lena had always adored. The sight was captivating, hypnotizing.

Only the sound of Rhea calling to her from the cash register could make Lena stop staring at a spot in the store anyone else would have seen as the mattress department. As shaken as Lena was, she was relieved to see that Rhea was back to normal. Yet on the way home, Lena could barely sit still. One minute she was overjoyed at the thought that Mom might actually be alive. The next she was terrified by the idea that Yarrow had found his way into her head. She'd have to tell....

But no, she must not even think of ... that one ... not now. The disaster looming on the horizon since August was closing in fast.

CHAPTER THIRTY-ONE

Anyone up at dawn the next morning would have heard a reckless driver gunning a powerful engine down deserted side streets where, in 1910, the Skudderton Lace factory had employed 48 local men and 12 women — most of whom had recently emigrated from France.

But as Blade Northrop zoomed past the boarded-up plant and its partially collapsed warehouse, he knew none of this. The only thing in his mind was the intoxicating thrill of going way over the speed limit. Careening around the corners in this ramshackle part of town was the only thing that cleared his head. With his heart racing and his knuckles gone white, Blade could finally remember who he ... used to be.

Something was wrong. Ever since that day at Harmony Beach, it was like he was walking inside his own ghost. He remembered a few pieces of his past, but mostly found himself living by rote, doing things not because they made sense but because they reminded him of a part of himself he knew he must have lost.

That's why he got up in the morning and why he walked upright on two legs and why — for reasons he couldn't grasp — he found himself staring at every girl he passed on the street. That is, he sort of remembered that pretty girls used to matter to him, but ... why?

There was really only one girl he could care about, wasn't that right? Callie ... Callie Ann ... and there was a familiar saying that echoed in his head whenever he thought of her.

"I'm going out with Callie Ann," Blade said for the hundredth time, as he roared up Trolley Lane to the back of the Skudderton Post Office where Yarrow was waiting for him.

Yarrow, he knew. Yarrow had given him this gunmetal gray Mazda Miata and a crazy amount of money. That part was cool. So why'd the Team Leader have to wreck everything by breaking Blade's trust?

"Work your ass off for a guy and he goes and clones you," muttered Blade as he slammed the driver's side door shut. "He's gonna hear about that," Blade added, lighting up a cigarette. Cigarettes still made sense, even if he couldn't remember why.

"Where have you been?" snarled the wiry man in the crushed velvet jumpsuit who greeted Blade inside what was left of the Skudderton post office.

Fortunately, one of the other things Blade remembered from ... before ... was that he was better off not answering most of Yarrow's questions.

"It's all set up," Blade replied, stubbing out his cigarette on the filthy vinyl tile beneath his boots. "Want to talk to you about ... about those things you made out of me."

Yarrow wasn't hearing it. Waving away Blade's complaints, Yarrow held out a package wrapped in a thin, metallic foil of nearly pure iridium and clapped Blade on the shoulder.

"This is the last one," he said. "I know I can trust only you to deliver it for me."

Nodding, Blade took the package, rolled it over in his hands and glanced back at Yarrow.

"So after this," he said, "I'm free, right? I mean, you can get plenty of help from those...."

"Get going," said Yarrow, shoving Blade out of his office. "We'll talk about your severance package when you finish."

Pausing long enough to light another cigarette, Blade stalked out to the parking lot, not realizing that the only "severance" Yarrow intended to pay out was the bloody kind.

All the same, once Blade was out in the parking lot, he knew in the back of his fragmentary thoughts that he must be in danger. Maybe it was the way the bright morning sun bounced off the top of his shiny new car, but in that moment, the reincarnated teenager saw he couldn't believe a word Yarrow said.

"We'll leave the girl out of it," Yarrow had promised Blade over and over again since the day he woke up in the transmog chamber. One way to make sure, Blade realized. He'd have to get Callie Ann into the Mazda with him, where'd she be safe. Then he'd drive her to a place far away, like Hawaii.

Even though Blade sensed there might be a piece missing in his plan to save Callie Ann, it felt good to know he was finally in control of his life again. That Yarrow dude? He was in for a surprise.

CHAPTER THIRTY-TWO

These days, Derek worked nonstop, keeping his body awake and alert with Snaldrialooran neuro-stimulators. But even though extra-terrestrial medical science could keep him going almost indefinitely, lack of sleep was eating away at his human personality. For his part, Derek was oblivious to the change that had come over him — but it was way obvious to Vance Maultsby.

"Would you just chill?" shouted Vance, as he threw down his mouse, grabbed the transmogged alien by his shirt collar and flung him to the floor. "I can't write code any faster with you complaining at me."

"I'm simply saying…. " Derek started.

"Yeah, well maybe if I did have eight blue tentacles I could type faster, but I don't," Vance yelled. "I don't!"

Vance released Derek from the grip of his large hands, stomped over to the glass patio doors and stared out at the half-acre plot, now dotted with clumps of onion grass and bright yellow dandelions.

"Sorry, Man," he said. "But I'm only…. "

"Nothing wrong with being human," said Derek, picking himself up from the living room's soft pile carpeting.

"Not what I meant," snapped Vance, turning on his heels. "I mean ... I'm only a kid, you gotta cut me some slack."

"Yarrow's activating the *kalthruth* in less than 36 hours," said Derek, looking up into Vance's horned rims. "After that, it won't matter how much of a jerk I am now."

"Right," said Vance, walking back over to the workstation he and Derek had brought back from the Snaldrialooran lander. "Remember that the next time you call me an idiot."

Staring at the back of Vance's head, Derek considered using mentallic persuasion, but rejected it. Not only could it derail the assault on the Vrukaari, it could also hurt one of only three people Derek counted as friends in this sector of the universe. He'd already risked enough by using a modified direct-to-cortex teaching module to enhance Vance's programming skills.

So while Vance settled back into adapting his Sim-like game to new specs, Derek collapsed on the sofa and stretched his mind out to Lena, hoping he could hold his attack plan together for one more day. With long practice, mentallic communication was a reflex for him, like blinking an eye or taking a breath — even if both sensations had been changed by the transmog process.

How he wished his accusers could know how horrible it was to live out your life in an alien body. They'd outlaw a form of punishment he could now only see, ironically, as "inhumane." Maybe, if he ever returned to the Homeworld, he'd deliver a speech to the....

Wait. Even at this distance, Derek could sense Yarrow's resistance field, shielding Lena's thoughts from any potential outside influence. That left him with a tough choice. Sure, he could smash through Yarrow's defenses and free Lena's mind, but not without showing his hand to the enemy.

Near as Derek could make out from his interception of Yarrow's transmissions, the Lieutenant Colonel still thought Derek was under the tight control of the Snaldrialooran prison robots. At the brink of Yarrow's deadly assault on Earth, that one delusion was the only thing protecting Derek's plan.

"All right," said Vance, slapping the workstation's stainless steel frame. "Check this out. I think I got it!"

Nodding at Vance, Derek didn't immediately jump up to join him. First, he needed to set a few gears in motion. Confusing Yarrow's sensors was only Phase One of his plan. To succeed, Derek would also have to halt the mass-transmog of the Vrukaari cells inside the mailboxes into fully formed soldiers.

Remembering his conversation with Jalgren Altrollinhar through the DXN units' transponder, Derek knew he had to strike hard at Yarrow's weakest link.

"The final trigger is entirely mentallic," his older cousin had said. "Don't ask me why. I'd never initiate such a delicate operation that way — too many variables."

"What do you mean?" Derek remembered asking.

"What do I ... Listen, even the most disciplined mind can't keep itself from wandering," the professor had said. "The tiniest distraction could derail the entire process. So instead of an army of soldiers, Yarrow could create an army of ... of sandwiches if he were hungry enough."

"So I have to distract Yarrow long enough to issue a substitute mental command?" Derek had asked.

"Not so easy," Jalgren had said. "The Vrukaari aren't stupid. Yarrow will issue the command through a transponder, to reduce the margin of error. To get a warrior mentality like Yarrow to flinch under those conditions, you'd have to strike at his greatest fear. You'll have to find *that* out for yourself."

What could it be, wondered Derek now, wishing he could push off from the couch and relieve the tension with a good swim.

"Dude, you've got to love this," said Vance as a grin spread over his broad face. "I programmed this whole sequence where the Post Office catches fire."

"How?" asked Derek.

"Gets hit by lightning," said Vance. "It's so cool."

"And you can initiate that sequence any time?" asked Derek, trying hard to stretch the tension out of his neck muscles.

"I set it to go off in a couple of days," said Vance, "but you could trigger it, whenever, with the mind thing you do, right?"

True enough, the Snaldrialooran device he'd brought over from the lander could respond to mentallic commands. Plus, Yarrow's transponder would be patched in directly to the sensory feed from the Vrukaari lander. If Derek fed Vance's simulated lightning strike to Yarrow's transponder at the exact right moment, he'd throw the enemy off his concentration.

Trouble was, Derek couldn't be in two places at once, mentallically speaking. Even if he could catch Yarrow off guard, another mind would have to complete the command sequence while the Vrukaari was distracted.

Looking down at his Adidas, he realized he'd have to rely on Lena, and in that moment saw exactly what he needed to do. His forehead pounding, he tried to work out a way to plant the seed for Yarrow's defeat in Lena's mind without her knowledge.

Now that he'd detected Yarrow's presence at the fringes of Lena's mind, Derek realized that even a nanosecond of doubt would allow the Vrukaari soldier to refocus his thoughts. Worse, Derek would have to reach Lena without mentallics. Lucky for him, there was a safer way to get through to her.

"Lena?" he said into his cell phone a minute later.

"You're *calling* me?" asked Lena from Dad's Touareg, on her way back from another exhausting mall-run with Rhea.

"I was wondering if you needed more Jell-O molds for the reception dinner," he said. "I found a couple in my pantry."

"Why would I need those?" asked Lena, her throat tightening.

"Well everyone knows how much you love that stuff," said Derek. "I just want to help you celebrate the wedding."

"This is so not ... like you," said Lena. "Did Vance put you up to this?"

"Just trying to help," said Derek, laughing. "So, I guess, no lime Jell-O at the reception?"

"No!" yelled Lena, hanging up on him.

And in that moment, Derek knew Lena's angry response had planted the mentallic trigger he needed into the deepest recesses of her mind. When this was over, he realized, he'd have to apologize for playing with her emotions. But for now....

"Perfect," said Derek, clutching a couch pillow close to his chest.

"You haven't even seen it yet," said Vance from across the room, pointing to his computer monitor.

"But I *know* it will be perfect," said Derek as he walked over to Vance's work station, "I have faith in you."

"Keep talking like that," said Vance with a smile, "and you'll turn into a real boy someday."

If Derek had been listening, he might have been insulted. But with the forces of Fate spinning around him, all he could think about was how to instruct Vance to program in the trigger mechanism he needed at the crucial moment. For the first time in weeks, he felt himself breathe easy. It was going to be close, but they just might make it.

CHAPTER THIRTY-THREE

Somehow, despite the buzzing in her ears, the creepy sense that she was being watched and the fleeting glimpses of Mom hovering at the edge of her vision, Lena managed to get through the day at school and help Dad and Rhea work out the final details of their wedding in the evenings. Not that she was much use, her mind wandering, as she fought to keep her thoughts off ... certain topics ... she didn't want ... someone ... to know about.

Lucky for her, the adults in her life wrote her behavior off to the shock of seeing her father remarry. While it bugged her to think they didn't know her better, Lena figured their misunderstanding was the best smoke screen she could hope for.

Besides, she had way more important things on her mind — like being cut off from her friends when they needed her most, when they were desperately afraid that ... but it was better not to go down that road. Better to focus on finalizing the floral arrangements that Rhea had designed herself.

How much easier this moment could have been, if not for ... recent events. The idea of Dad getting married would still have shaken her up, but Lena had decided early on that Rhea was good for him.

By this point, Lena realized, she should have been able to focus on the sheer fun of preparing a wedding — and the excuses it gave her to bug out on field hockey practice. Instead, she was too busy waiting for the slightest sign that ... her friends ... might need help with their ... Science project. Worried as she was, she only allowed herself a split-second glimpse at Vance's mind, hoping it was still free of outside influence.

To conceal her thoughts, Lena decided to use a mentallic technique she'd recently learned from ... the boy.

And as it happened, her stepmom-to-be had made it easy for her. Rhea had asked Lena to go over the receipts for the wedding expenses so far, suspecting the caterer was double billing for a few of the less inexpensive items. As boring as it was, this was exactly the kind of mental drudgery she needed to shield....

"Focus," Lena said aloud. "These receipts are important." Meanwhile, she used the deeper recesses of her mind for telepathy.

By now, she saw, Vance must have completed his work on the Sim-like game environment he'd designed. That was the only explanation for the shimmering glow she detected on the outer surface of his mind. Though she dared not delve deeper — who knew what gross guy stuff she'd find? — that was the only one possible explanation.

That could only mean ... her friends ... were almost ready to roll. From her brief flash of contact with Derek, in the form of last night's unusually vivid dreams, Lena knew her part in the project would become clear when the time came.

Yeah, right. If any one word could describe the last three months of her life, "clarity" wasn't it. Still, better stay positive. Of all the ways she could let her friends down, giving up was the worst.

Though it was comforting to sense the confidence in Derek's mind, it amazed Lena to think how much was riding on scientific concepts she had known nothing about last summer and barely understood now. If she ever got out of this mess, she decided, she'd have to start reading up.

Meanwhile, the preparations for the wedding, and the emotions that swirled around them, were ratcheting up to high gear. In 24 hours, she'd be watching Dad and Rhea get hoisted up on chairs before a crowd of excited family and friends.

Ironically, Lena kept obsessing over the idea of how thrilled Mom would have been to see the occasion, to see Dad so happy, except ... except....

"Oh, Lena, Dear, of course I'm happy for your father," the syrupy imitation of Mom's voice now echoed in Lena's mind. "That's why I don't want you doing things with your scruffy new friends to make him ashamed of you."

"Ashamed of me?" asked Lena. That settled it. Mom had been very persuasive when she wanted to be, and forceful when she needed to be, but she had never — never — played with Lena's feelings like that.

"You know I'm right," said the hallucination, with an inflection scarily close to the real thing.

"I know you're a fake!" shouted Lena without realizing it. The next minute, there was Dad in the threshold of her room, his head tilted, his eyes wide and inquisitive.

"Sorry," said Lena, blushing. "I've had a Dark Matter song running through my head all day."

"Some song," said Dad. "You almost finished there?" he added.

"Yeah. Reminds me of doing the receipts for the tour boat," said Lena. "I'm gonna miss that," she sighed.

"Why?" asked Dad with a smile. "You have plans for the summer?"

"You mean you'll still…." said Lena.

"Wrote it into the marriage vows," whispered Dad, kissing her on the forehead. A minute later he was gone, but Lena still lingered in that moment. Despite everything, she felt like the luckiest girl in Skudderton. That is, until Arkansas' insistent meowing at his dish broke in on her thoughts. Funny thing was, even though the whole planet hung in the balance, Lena was no less worried about what might happen to her fuzzy-faced feline than she was about saving humanity.

And, as she reflected on her way to the kitchen cabinets to get him a can of "Hearty Kitty Meow-ness-trone," the day of reckoning was coming up fast. Blaring on the TV in the living room, where Dad sat snuggled up to Rhea, a newsreader spoke in grave tones about a mysterious late night assault on a small party of eco-tourists in Zamora, Ecuador.

The more details tumbled out of the TV, the more the story reminded Lena of the mentallic images Derek had shown her of the fishing village in Nova Scotia the week before. The ... bad guys ... she realized, were steadily testing their gear. It was almost time!

CHAPTER THIRTY-FOUR

It was late morning the following day before Derek and Vance had loaded their equipment into a gym bag, dragged it out to Callie Ann's 2001 Corolla, and rolled their eyes while she struggled to get it started.

"Loser!" she screamed, as it stalled out again.

Derek flinched as her fist came down hard on the dashboard. His first instinct was to consult the Galactic Array for the phone number of the nearest mechanic. But Vance acted first.

"Get out," he growled, pawing at the rear seat door handle, "we have to push."

"All the way to Harmony Beach?" asked Derek, hesitating a bit before climbing out on the other side. But he was pleasantly surprised. After a few feet of pushing — mostly by Vance — the engine revved up and stuttered back to life.

"How could this possibly work?" asked Derek, eyes wide.

"Pushing it turns the gear box," said Vance, with a shrug. "You pop the clutch, the engine thinks you sparked it, you go."

"I'm pretty sure the engine doesn't think," said Derek, still perplexed.

"It's just a ... like ... a metaphor, right?" asked Callie Ann, as she pulled out of Derek's driveway.

"I got the engine started," grumbled Vance, "that's enough for me. What I *want* to know is why you're driving a stick shift in the first place."

"My Dad," sighed Callie Ann. "He wants me to learn about cars. Like that's going to happen."

"Can we get moving?" asked Derek, tilting his head in the direction of the highway. The temptation to force the issue mentallically was....

"Dude," said Vance, flashing a grin, "don't go all Jedi mind tricks on us. We're ready to go."

Closing his eyes as Callie Ann pulled away from the curb, Derek wondered how it was possible that sentient minds with no sign of mentallic abilities had still managed to imagine them in vivid detail.

Could it be the next to last step in an evolutionary development leading to....

"You want to tell me what we're doing when we get there?" asked Callie Ann, pursing her lips. "I mean ... can you help Blainy get better, or not?"

And though Derek was determined to leave Callie Ann's mind untouched, he couldn't help noticing how close she had come to ending her sentence with "you little creep." Lena would never think that, he realized, as he held his head in his hands.

But this was not the time for sulking and he set himself the difficult task of bringing Callie Ann up to date with the current state of the crisis — without scaring her to death.

"You buying this, Vance?" asked Callie Ann, glancing into the rear-view mirror.

Lucky for Derek, Vance had seen the inside of the Snaldrialooran lander. So between the two of them, by the time Callie Ann was on the exit ramp for Harmony Beach, she knew enough to realize how much more was at stake than saving her boyfriend.

"You don't even know if this will work, do you?" she asked, as they pulled into Parking Lot 4. A moment later, they were heading for the sand when a uniformed patrolman drove up in a squad car and gestured for them to stop.

"Don't you kids have school?" asked the heavyset officer, his face grim.

"Exam week," said Vance with a shrug. "You know how it is."

"Don't think I do," snapped the patrolman. "Anyway, doesn't matter. This beach is off limits."

"Why?" asked Derek as meekly as he could, considering his mind was about to explode.

"Quarantined," the officer said. "Something's sticking out of the sand even the scientists haven't seen before. Whole beach is closed, so you better get home and ... study for exams, or whatever."

Just as Vance opened his mouth to protest, the patrolman's walkie-talkie squawked a brief message and he drove off, leaving Derek only a split second to jump clear of his radial tires.

"Sounds like they found the *kalthruth*," said Derek squeezing his eyes shut.

"You think?" asked Vance. "How are we going to install my program if we can't get close enough?"

But that was only one of the problems Derek saw, as he peered into the aerial view he'd picked up through the Galactic Array. Now that the beach was crawling with humans, Yarrow would have an incentive to strike sooner rather than later — before the Earth people had a chance to damage his buried power station.

"I have an idea," he said, "but we'll need to drive south and re-enter the beach away from the park entrance."

Callie Ann stared at him briefly and then jumped back into the driver's seat.

"What are you thinking?" she demanded, once they were on the road again.

As Derek explained, the police and the large party from the FBI were so preoccupied with the part of the *kalthruth* sticking out from the sand — the part Callie Ann had excavated the day before — that it would be hours before they realized the truth: The Vrukaari energy station extended far out to sea.

In fact, most of its mass was underwater, connected by a wireless metadigital interface to the Vrukaari lander, which Derek guessed must be no more than 15 miles off shore.

"Fifteen miles?" said Vance, his voice trailing off in the wind from the ocean. "How are we gonna.... "

"We won't have to go that far out, Dumbass," said Callie Ann. "Am I right?" she added, catching Derek's eye in the rearview mirror.

"Right," Derek replied, grateful he didn't have to say too much more. With so many law-enforcement personnel converging on the *kalthruth*, he had to put more energy into monitoring the mentallic "airways," looking as discreetly as possible for signs that Yarrow was ready to risk a premature strike.

At last, the three of them reached a point along the highway that Derek decided was far enough away to give them cover, but not too far to put the alien device out of reach. Urging his friends to silence, he motioned for Vance to help him gather their gear from the trunk of the car.

As they hurried down to the beach, clambering over a stretch of low-lying, shattered dune fence, his whispered instructions to Callie Ann brought a faraway look to her jade-green eyes.

"I guess I can do it," she said, as they crept down to the edge of the water. "Should have brought a snorkel."

"If you don't think you can...." Derek sputtered.

"Didn't say that, dork-face," said Callie Ann. "Now turn around, both of you."

Seconds later, Derek heard the splash of ocean water behind him as Callie Ann plunged into the water wearing only ... no, better keep his mind on the mission. One slip of his thoughts was all Yarrow would need. After what felt like hours....

"I'm back," panted Callie Ann behind him.

"How did it.... " said Vance.

"Just get up to the car as fast as you can and I'll join you," she said, catching her breath. "I think someone saw me."

And as Derek and Vance scrambled back up the dune to the car, a megaphone rang out behind them.

"Young Lady," a stern voice boomed, "stay right where you are."

"What do we do?" asked Vance, reaching out a powerful arm to help Derek the rest of the way up the dune.

"We keep moving," said Derek. "The way I figure it, we only have three hours left before.... "

"OK, don't say it," said Vance, jumping into the driver's seat of the car. "Just give me a push so we can get out of here."

"You're kidding, right?" asked Derek, more out of breath than at any time since coming to Earth.

"Duh," said Vance with a grin. "She left the keys on the seat."

Glancing back at the ocean, Derek could barely catch the outline of Callie Ann in the harsh mid-morning sunlight, as she scrambled to gather her clothes and run up the dune to join them.

"Whoa," said Vance, grabbing Derek's chin and pivoting his head away from the beach. "She catches you looking, you're in for a world of hurt."

Still dazed from running uphill for the first time on human legs, Derek complied without fully understanding. Seconds later, the rear passenger door opened and Callie Ann jumped in behind him, clutching her soaking wet shirt around her.

"Turn around and you're dead!" she yelled.

Meanwhile, the booming voice in the megaphone kept up its insistent rant.

"This is Agent Holland, FBI," it railed. "Give yourself up now and we won't press charges."

"Just drive," said Derek in a low voice as Callie Ann slammed her door shut, lurching forward as Vance got the motor running and spun out onto the highway.

"Think we made it in time?" asked Callie Ann a moment later, grabbing Derek by the shoulders.

"Don't know," said Derek in a monotone.

Shaking her head, Callie Ann slammed herself back into her seat and ran her fingers through her fine blond hair over and over again.

"What about Lena?" she asked, as Vance barreled on like a NASCAR driver.

"Exactly," said Derek, his eyes glazed over.

"Dude, you OK?" asked Vance, without turning his head.

"Have to ... to ... have to concentrate," said Derek. And as the highway opened up in front of him, he felt a new wave of dread seep into his bones. Trouble was coming up fast.

CHAPTER THIRTY-FIVE

The day of the wedding was already in progress when Lena glimpsed the first signs of trouble. Glimpsed, that is, out at the fringes of her consciousness. And though she didn't understand why, like an optical illusion you can only grasp indirectly, she knew:

Something was horribly wrong.

Worse, with the excitement swirling around her, and her heart racing with bittersweet happiness for Dad, it was even more difficult than usual to know what to do about the strange situation she found herself in.

If there was any way she could help ... her friends ... she would. But all she had to do was wonder how and her thoughts clouded over again. In the absence of a worked-out plan, she knew she might easily do more harm than good. As ... the boy ... had explained many times, mentallic communication was instantaneous and those who mastered it could react with reflexes faster than she could imagine.

Better wait, she decided, for the unmistakable signal Derek had promised her in her dreams. For if the situation had progressed to the point where there was no hope of receiving such a signal, then....

For now, she dared not follow this dark train of thought; its presence could itself send a signal, a fatal clue to a plan that might still succeed, if only....

"Moping, again?" asked Rhea's voice from across the room. "Come on, cheer up," she added, walking over to Lena's bed where she sat, her bridesmaid's gown laid out in front of her. "I'll take good care of him."

"Oh hi," said Lena, willing an air of wistful cheer to enter her voice. "I was trying to remember if I put the gladioli in the right place for the reception."

"You don't have to be so brave," said Rhea, as she gave Lena a hug. "Like I don't know what's running through your mind."

"You know?" said Lena, her chest tightening.

"Went through the exact same thing with my father," said Rena, straightening a couple of stray locks in Lena's hair. "Except *my* stepmother was a witch."

"Must have ... must have been tough," said Lena. Funny thing was, she couldn't tell what mattered more, that her secret was safe or that Rhea cared enough to share part of her life story.

"Limo's here!" Dad shouted excitedly, from downstairs. Lena and Rhea hurried to the window as the stretch limo Todd Gabrilowicz had ordered for his wedding came crunching up the driveway.

"Way to wreck the mood," Lena mumbled.

Grinning, Rhea shouted down the stairwell at Dad, then turned to help Lena struggle into her frilly peach-colored bridesmaid's gown. Lena couldn't help but smile, both at the tremble she'd heard in Dad's voice and at the common sense suggestions Rhea made about her hair.

It ought to have been one of the happiest moments of Lena's life, and it would have been — except for the hallucination of Mom that lingered, scowling at the edge of Lena's line of sight.

"You could have lost a little weight in time for the wedding," her voice echoed in Lena's mind.

Though it was tempting to lash out, either verbally, which would have frightened Rhea, or mentallically, which would have ruined everything, Lena held her ground and focused instead on the look of acceptance on Rhea's face. Lena knew exactly who Mom was — who Mom had been — and this apparition was not her. Ironically, it was Rhea, Mom's "replacement" who helped Lena find the courage to resist.

"I don't think I've ever seen you look so pretty," Rhea said, as the two of them stood in front of Lena's mirror. That is, until Dad's stuttering voice on the stairs made them nearly jump out of their skins.

All the way to the wedding, Lena was torn between the happiness radiating from her heart, and the dark, subterranean thoughts that snaked through her mind. The entire mentallic field surrounding ... her friends ... was distorted, misshapen, which was as much as she could perceive without delving deeper and giving herself away.

Though she was caught up in the excitement of the wedding and determined not to let this day get spoiled, she knew she'd have to take action. But how, when and, by the way, what action? She'd have to trust her instincts. Trouble was, she didn't exactly *have* any instinct for intergalactic war. Before she met Derek, Lena's biggest conflict in life had been keeping Arkansas off the kitchen table when she was making tuna salad.

But look, there was Aunt Kathy — all stiff and uncomfortable in her formal gown — tugging on the passenger side door handle, ready to help her out of the limo. Later for the saving the planet thing: The moment had arrived!

CHAPTER THIRTY-SIX

Out on a deserted stretch of highway between Skudderton and Harmony Beach, Derek jammed his right hand into the dashboard in front of him as Vance swerved Callie Ann's Corolla into the shoulder and stomped on the brakes.

"You believe this?" yelled Vance, glaring at the improbable sight through the windshield.

Derek sat motionless, his jaw tense. He'd seen nothing on the Galactic Array to prepare him for this: A line of 12 teenage boys in front of them, standing shoulder to shoulder across both lanes, each one wearing Blade Northrop's face.

"Blainy?" said Callie Ann, leaning forward to peer through the windshield.

"Clones," said Derek, his lip trembling.

"Why is that possible?" asked Vance. "OK, stupid question."

"Good ... question," said Derek, breaking out into a sweat. "No time for answer."

"So what do we...." Vance began.

"Distract them," said Derek. "Have to get back ... Skudderton ... or...."

"OK, I got this," said Callie Ann. Before Vance could stop her, Callie Ann had jumped out of the car and was heading straight for the wall of Blade clones in front of them.

"What's she doing?" said Vance, reaching to open his door. That is, until Derek's hand shot out to grab Vance's wrist.

"Wait," said Derek, his glazed eyes staring straight ahead through the windshield. "Think I know what she's ... what she'll do."

Shaking his head, but unable to break free of Derek's surprisingly strong grip, Vance watched Callie Ann strut past the line of clones, pausing in front of every third one to purr,

"Why don't you ditch these losers, so we can go someplace nice and ... be *alone* for a while?"

Taking up position about halfway between the Blade clones and her car, she waited with her arms folded across her chest, breathing hard. At first, nothing much happened, as if the clones hadn't even noticed

Callie Ann. The shift came soon after, as each of the four she had whispered to turned sharp and punched the clone on his right in the stomach.

Vance cringed at the sight of 12 Blade Northrop's punching, kicking, slamming each other into the pavement, in a bout fierce enough to make last season's X-Treme Fighting Championship look like his baby sister's third birthday party. Callie Ann looked on, covering her eyes as the brutal slugfest continued, meanwhile edging closer and closer to the rear door of her car. At last, Vance, having finally peeled Derek's fingers from his wrist, reached back and opened the rear door.

"Get in," he said in a hoarse whisper, and as Callie Ann slammed the door shut behind her, Vance edged the Corolla's scratched front fender out of the shoulder. The car lurched forward as Vance floored it, zooming down the highway in the left lane, then swerving over to the right, once they were past the fierce melee of arms, fists, teeth, and legs behind them.

"You did that, didn't you?" asked Callie Ann, poking Derek in the shoulder once the clones were safely out of sight.

"You did," said Derek, "I just ... intensified."

"Did what?" asked Vance.

"You don't want to know," said Callie Ann, pulling her shirt tight around her.

"So, Dude, what next?" asked Vance, clenching his jaw.

"Skudderton," said Derek. "Faster."

And hearing the quiet intensity in Derek's voice, Vance jammed his foot down on the gas pedal and left it there.

"You nuts?" shouted Callie Ann. "We'll crash ... or get pulled over by the cops."

But for the remainder of their road trip, they saw no other cars on the road, police or otherwise. As they veered to the right for the exit ramp, Vance's eyes opened wide.

"You keeping all the cars away?" he asked in a low voice.

"Faster," said Derek.

"Where?" demanded Callie Ann. "If I'm going to die, I want to know what for."

"Post office," said Derek.

"You expecting a package?" asked Callie Ann, throwing her arms in the air.

"That's where the bad guys are," said Vance.

"You mean those mailboxes," said Callie Ann. "Makes sense. Blainy's been mumbling about mailboxes and delivering packages ever since he started with that creepy Yarrow guy."

"You've ... met Yarrow?" asked Derek, turning around in his seat to face her.

"Couple times, before Blainy disappeared," said Callie Ann. "Creep came to my house looking for him. Tried to touch me. Can you believe that?"

"Would you recognize him if...." Derek's voice cracked.

"Totally," said Callie Ann, wrinkling her nose. "It's like he burned his face right into my brain."

Derek sank back into his seat and withdrew into himself. The Vrukaari soldier had already entered her mind!

CHAPTER THIRTY-SEVEN

Blade Northrop squinted against the late afternoon sun as he steered his gunmetal gray Mazda Miata along the meticulously landscaped boulevards that swept through the Hunter's Wend section of town.

"Figures," he grunted, gazing out at Derek's semi-exclusive neighborhood.

All the real jerks in the world were the rich jerks, he told himself — and from what he'd learned about Derek from Callie Ann, the new kid would fit right in here.

The proof? Mr. Yarrow had told Blade to deliver a package right to Derek's door. That meant Derek was a threat to The Plan. Making a sharp left, Blade sneered at the clumps of mailboxes marring every block, even here, where plenty of people had connections to government circles.

Trouble was, even the Feds wouldn't touch the mailboxes — for reasons Blade thought only he and Yarrow knew. But much as he enjoyed feeling like an insider, it bugged him to think he could never earn the alien Lieutenant Colonel's complete trust.

What was up with that? If the Team Leader could put Blade's life at risk to deliver these packages, how come he couldn't tell Blade the whole story? Besides, *this* package wasn't anything like the others he'd delivered, including the one at Harmony Beach.

That was the trouble with Yarrow.

"Too many secrets," Blade grumbled into his steering wheel.

Like those crappy clones the guy had made without even asking. Who knew what else he was hiding? His arm tensing, Blade yanked on the emergency brake, reached back into the tiny passenger seat and grabbed the shiny metal package he was supposed to slide under Derek's front door. In the process, he caught a glimpse in his side mirror of a well-groomed miniature collie, trotting down the sidewalk towards his car.

Turning the gleaming package over in his hands, Blade made up his mind. No way he was taking orders from a guy who lied to him. The Team? The Plan? Later for that. Blade Northrop had a plan of his own, starting with Step One: Ditch this package and go get Callie Ann.

Blade stopped long enough to light a cigarette, rolled down his window and tossed the shiny, silvery-white package out onto the sidewalk — and into the mouth of the collie who, despite the urgent clapping of her well-mannered owner, had run right up to the Mazda's wheels.

Wasting no time, Blade backed out of the driveway and, with no regard for the neighbor's curbside hydrangeas, zoomed off in the direction he came. Focused with the obsessive zeal of a disgruntled employee, Blade never thought to check his rearview mirror. Otherwise, he would have witnessed the convulsive agony of the collie and her owner — as toxic gas, subliming rapidly from the super-cooled liquid inside the package, seeped into their gasping lungs.

Nor would Blade have appreciated the touch of irony Relsheesharb Yarrow had built into his murder plans. What better tool to terminate a transmogged Snaldrialooran than a dose of the Homeworld atmosphere his human body could no longer tolerate?

Roaring away at 70 mph through the spacious, winding streets of Derek's neighborhood, Blade's anger forced the package from his thoughts. But to Derek, whose mind had been hovering at the edge of Blade's consciousness ever since Lena had described the lanky teenager's zombie-like reappearance, the iridium-foil package read as a final warning sign.

Combined with the appearance of the clones, Blade's deadly mission meant Yarrow was nearly ready to strike. Arriving at the ruined Skudderton post office with Vance and Callie Ann, he knew he had to prepare himself for the final stages of his plan — whether the moment came in nine hours or a nano-second from now.

But wait. Maybe Yarrow's attempt on his life was standard Vrukaari military procedure: kill every potential adversary. Or had Derek's plan been compromised by the thin thread of mentallic energy connecting Yarrow to Callie Ann?

Either way, Yarrow wanted him dead.

Worse, as Derek learned from the Galactic Array, his own time on Earth was running out. The Snaldrialooran starspanner, on its way to arrest him, had already entered Earth's solar system. If he was going to stop the Vrukaari, it had to be soon, before Homeworld authorities took him away to stand trial a second time — and condemned an entire planetary population to death.

As space-time converged on the tipping point of the crisis, Derek wondered where he would find the courage to ... but no, there was no question of that. He'd been brave and stupid enough to steal government secrets and sell them to Ambassador Ghaar. No way he wasn't just as brave — and stupid — now to make up for his crime and save the humans from ... from....

It was too horrible to imagine, even in the abstract symbols that made up the mentallic landscape he must now navigate with the utmost caution.

"So, what now?" asked Vance, clapping Derek on the shoulder.

"We wait," said Derek.

"What? What for? I can't wait around here after I've seen that ... that thing in the sand," yelled Callie Ann.

"Keep your voice down," said Derek, slumping deep into his seat as if he were expecting a missile attack. "Now listen," he added, "I've been meaning to ask you. Have you and Blade ever ... you know...."

Callie Ann's mind flooded with rage and indignation, and in that moment Derek infiltrated her thoughts, hoping her violent emotions would mask his presence and enable him to widen the mentallic pipeline that linked her thoughts to Yarrow's, undetected.

"You creep!" yelled Callie Ann, raising her hand to slap him across the face.

"Cut it out," said Vance, his voice steady as he reached out to grab her forearm. "Dude said that for a good reason. Tell me you did," he added, his eyes fixed on Derek, "so I don't have to slap you myself."

"You're right," said Derek, "but don't ask me to explain."

"It's OK, I already knew you were a jerk." said Callie Ann. "Would you let go of me?" she snapped at Vance. "So what now?"

And as Vance released his grip, his eyes still trained on her hands, Derek turned around in his seat and faced Callie Ann, seeing her for the first time without a trace of infatuation.

"Think you can get into the wedding reception?" he asked.

"Now?" asked Vance, starting the engine.

As they veered out of the post office parking lot, Derek told Callie Ann the urgent message he needed her to give Lena.

"Are you serious?" asked Callie Ann, her eyes squinting shut. But the look on Derek's face when she opened her eyes told her how deadly serious he was.

"OK," said Callie Ann, as Vance steered her silver Corolla down Trolley lane, away from the ruined post office and out toward her neighborhood, "but I better get a ride in a spaceship out of this."

"I'll make a few calls," sighed Derek, watching the streets of Skudderton with his human eyes, while the eyes of his Snaldrialooran mentallic field scanned Callie Ann's thoughts for the slightest fluctuation in her personality vectors.

CHAPTER THIRTY-EIGHT

"Izshaarctrialoor!" growled Lieutenant Colonel Yarrow as he looked down at the vast, intricate control panel in front of him. Gathering intelligence on reams of release pods spread out across the planet would have been difficult under normal circumstances.

But between nagging mentallic static and intermittent, unexplained data dropouts, monitoring the transmog units and fine-tuning their settings was beginning to tax his strength. The enhanced access to the Galactic Array the Lander Team had patched together could only help him so much. He wasn't even sure it was worth the bullying it had required.

Not that threats and intimidation didn't have a charm all their own. But now, the Lander Team's most recent reports were wrecking his mood. A Snaldrialooran starspanner had just entered Earth's solar system, having appeared on the long range scanners out by the planet the humans referred to as "Neptune."

What did the Snaldrialooran hypocrites want? At a distance of 4.4 billion kilometers it was impossible to tell what class of ship they'd sent. Was it a battle cruiser, a diplomatic envoy vessel — or a group of bored, aristocratic tourists, hoping to amuse themselves by watching the battle for Earth at a safe distance?

Fine, he'd give them a show they could treasure the rest of their lives. But what if it was a military vessel? Would those self-righteous freaks of nature dare to compromise his mission?

Trying to control his rage, Yarrow realized the Snaldrialooran ship posed a serious threat he'd have to meet with cunning. His own government had refused to give him the firepower he requested when he received his orders, since the mission had been launched with the highest level of secrecy. In retrospect, a pair of battle cruisers would have drawn too much attention to the mission and almost certainly given away his position.

And yet, here he was without the cruisers, and his location had been compromised anyway. How was that possible? It was one thing for his enemies to discover the leaked documents and draw accurate conclusions about the use to which they might be put.

But how could they have discovered his base of operations in this unexplored sector of the universe? Until recently, he'd seen the arrival of the Snaldrialooran prisoner as a bizarre, yet harmless coincidence. The prisoner was no older than the Earth creature Yarrow himself had recruited and, by every indication, had no military training.

What if, on the other hand, there had always been more to the picture? If Pertahru Daherek's son were a military operative in disguise ... well, there was no sense in taking chances. That's why he'd ordered that shiftless Earth boy to finish Ixdahan off with a souvenir of his Homeworld.

By now, Yarrow reflected, his reincarnated recruit should have returned to collect his pay. Money was, after all, the only thing that motivated him. The threat of violence had merely made Blade Northrop defiant — as if he were numb to physical force, or had figured out how indispensable he was to Yarrow's operation.

Yet why, the gruff soldier wondered, had so much of this mission revolved around children? Aside from his human operative there was the Snaldrialooran brat and the Earth girl that High Command had needlessly infected only moments after entering Earth's atmosphere. Of the first two he was certain — wasn't he?

Checking the sensor input from the Lander Team, he breathed deep. Yes, the Earth boy was returning from his last delivery. The Snaldrialooran, he could see clearly, was still in the grip of the advanced artificial intelligences who acted as his jailers — and would soon be asphyxiated by the methane gas escaping from Blade's "special delivery" package. What delicious retribution for the trouble his people had caused the Vrukaari High Command over the centuries.

And as for the Earth girl, Lena, his own mentallic link was as strong as ever. He'd found her unique vulnerability with ease, as her thoughts hovered relentlessly over the memory of her deceased female parental.

If only he'd been able to get a more powerful hold on the other child in the equation, Blade's would-be consort. But she had proven strong-willed, her mind a turbulent ocean of chaotic neuro-electric activity — synapses firing in erratic pulses of a kind he had encountered only in battlefield conditions.

Too bad. Once her species was destroyed, the galaxy would lose a precious military asset. Properly trained, cloned in great enough numbers, an army of soldiers with a mentality like hers would be a great asset to the Vrukaari military. The way she had evaded the team of clones he had sent to retrieve her ... her death would mean the end of a badly-needed genetic resource.

Yet none of this speculation, he realized, had any impact on the success of his mission. Not when his troops were in place, the *kalthruth* had almost reached maximum capacity and only routine cross-checks stood between him and the final mentallic command sequence.

Once his assault was launched, let the hideous, tentacled prudes file as many legal briefs with the Interstellar Consortium as they wanted. By the time their first case emerged from the vast ocean of legal detritus the Consortium sifted through every rotation, it would be too late. Cleansed of sub-sentient vermin and properly re-engineered, Earth would become a valuable addition to the glorious Vrukaari Federation of Independent Planets.

More important, he, Lieutenant Colonel Relsheesharb Yarrow, would receive full credit for enriching his superiors. Why, the amount of Gadolinium available in the crust of Earth's outsized moon was more than enough to justify the mission. But the real prize was the advance foothold this conquest would give the Vrukaari in the Remote Regions.

While the Consortium, at the urging of the Snaldrialoorans, continued to dither over issues of "sovereignty," the Vrukaari would strike, dominate and control. It was, in Yarrow's mind, only fitting. Success belonged to the strong, the ruthless and the unsentimentally honest. If the self-righteous idiots got their tentacles in a twist it was no concern of his. Inside of an hour, he'd be drinking in the sweet air of conquest.

Smiling at that thought, he slapped the ergonomically adapted transponder headgear onto his ugly, transmogged skull and reached out with his mind to the lander's data stream.

"*Archialahzorn*," he grunted, as deep furrows etched themselves into his brow.

A meteorological event was brewing on the horizon. He didn't remember seeing that on his own sensors even half an hour before. Still, the reading from the Lander Team's sensor array was unmistakable. An electrostatically charged mass of atmospheric gas at subnormal pressures was moving straight toward his spatio-temporal coordinates.

Clicking his tongue, the stoic warrior found the idea of being struck by an electrical discharge of such high voltage rather unnerving.

As he adjusted his headgear, Yarrow noticed a slight tremble in his hands and made a mental note. One of his first acts as military governor of Earth would be to establish stringent atmospheric controls. Living at the mercy of planetary weather? It was a degree of barbarism unfit for a war hero — least of all, the triumphant slayer of millions on Shreshgelsnard 5.

CHAPTER THIRTY-NINE

Vance did his best to stay calm, as Derek, guided by the Galactic Array, led him on a roundabout route to Callie Ann's house. Derek insisted it was their best chance to avoid detection.

"Dude, don't we have like a ... a time limit for getting this done?" Vance asked, as he swerved up Union street and down around the First Presbyterian Church of Skudderton.

"We have time," said Derek, staring straight in front of him. "I can't appear to be in too much of a hurry, as if I were anticipating something."

"I thought you said that Yarrow guy couldn't ... hear you, or whatever," said Callie Ann, leaning forward in her seat.

"Still have to be careful," said Derek. "Besides, you need time to figure out what to tell Lena."

"You told me what to say," snarled Callie Ann. "Too bad it makes no sense."

They drove in silence, past faceless antique shops, tattered book stores, forlorn car dealerships and dingy real estate offices.

"Yo, where to now?" said Vance, his jaw tensing. "I'm gonna run out of gas.'

"Tell him," said Derek, turning back to look at Callie Ann again, trying to remember why he'd found her so attractive.

But instead of mulling it over any further, Derek used this opportunity, while her thoughts were focused on the route, to peer through the window he'd created into Yarrow's mind. Lucky for Derek, the Vrukaari soldier was much too preoccupied with the intricacies of his command module to notice.

As far as the Snaldrialooran exile could tell, the moment of truth might arrive at any time. Too bad nothing in Derek's previous experience had prepared him for this moment.

Not that a similar opportunity had ever presented itself: to negotiate life on an alien planet in an alien body — and see the day when seven billion sentient creatures might be massacred overnight?

Time was, his biggest worry was collecting enough credit tiles to buy a new high tide wardrobe, and most of his energy went to impressing the slender, slithering females at the Continuum Center — or catching the attention of Edahen Tricebehat, the hottest prize at Gahaldoronek Prep, the girl whose mentallic shimmer made rational thought dangerously difficult to maintain....

"Dude, wake up!" Vance's voice cut into Derek's daydreams. "We're here now. Is it OK for Callie Ann to...?"

Derek ripped himself away from his memory, cursing himself. His indirect contact with Yarrow through Callie Ann's mind had distracted him from his plan — and nearly revealed his position.

At Derek's request, Vance had parked about half a block away from Callie Ann's house, where a large forsythia bush gave them partial cover — at least where its leaves hadn't already tumbled to the sidewalk.

"Yes, go on," said Derek to Callie Ann, "and don't worry," he added, "I know you'll be great."

"Thanks," said Callie Ann, squeezing her athletic body out of the Corolla's cramped back seat. "But get this straight: I'm only doing this for Lena."

"She really hates me," said Derek, when Callie Ann had slammed the door behind her.

"Naw, she's scared," said Vance. "I mean, aren't you?" he added after a moment of silence. "You ever done anything like this before?"

"No," said Derek. "No matter how you define 'this' I've never done it before."

Vance peered out through the windshield. "Used to be," he said, "about the bravest thing I could see myself doing was asking a girl like Celia Roberts out to the Prom. Now my big dream is waking up on my 18th birthday." He leaned and peered out through the windshield. "Yo!" he cried, shooting a glance at the sky.

"What?" said Derek, as he tried to sense Lena's mentallic field through Yarrow's static.

"Am I trippin'," said Vance, pointing at the windshield, "or is that, like, a spaceship up there?"

Following the trajectory suggested by Vance's pointing finger, Derek glanced up at the sky and felt his stomach heave.

Wise Heralds of the Transdimensional Interface!

The Snaldrialooran starspanner had arrived too soon. Who knew how their well-meaning interference could jeopardize Derek's fragile assault plan, a strategy requiring more delicate timing than anything ever conceived on Earth?

Extending his mentallic field as far as he dared, Derek did his best to assess whether the envoy from the Homeworld had pinpointed his exact location. With luck, he could shield his mind from sensors on both the Homeworld mother ship and its lander — but not forever. One slip of the neuron and they'd spot him, come crashing down to make the arrest and leave this backward people to be decimated by Yarrow's invasion force.

"How long does she need to change her clothes?" Derek asked Vance in a hoarse whisper.

"She's a girl, Man," said Vance, drumming his fingers into the steering wheel. "Go figure. How long does it take girls to get dressed where you're from?"

But Derek wasn't paying attention. The Snaldrialooran ship, though still only a tiny speck in the sky would soon be detected by the Earth-bound observers, unless ... oh, but it was already masking its signal and....

There. It had cloaked itself, realizing how foolish it would be to reveal its position to a species with only the most limited knowledge of the universe. Why, Derek wondered, had the Snaldrialooran captain been so slow to analyze human signal traffic and see what had struck him almost immediately? Humans at these time coordinates had barely reached the second rung of the technological ladder.

"Ladder?" The question echoed through his thoughts. "What use would a ladder be to an eight-legged species gliding through liquid methane?"

Funny how this alien language carried its alien frame of reference with it. Even though Derek knew better, he couldn't stop himself from using human imagery when speaking a human language. Someday, he promised himself, he'd look into the relationship between language and culture more closely.

Right at this moment, he had a more immediate problem — like how to control what felt like the very forces of History swirling around him.

"Where'd they go?" asked Vance, shaking Derek by the shoulders. "Come on, tell me what's going down — I'm losing it over here."

"Try to stay calm." said Derek, fearing Vance's emotional outburst would attract the attention of a least one, if not both, of the extra-terrestrial mentalities he most wanted to avoid. Worse, the arrival of the Snaldrialooran ship meant Yarrow was likely to strike within the hour. Once the ship found Derek, every last piece of Derek's plan would have to be in place — but what was taking Callie Ann so long?

Frustrated as Derek was, if he'd seen what Callie Ann had seen a moment ago, he might have given up completely. She'd been brushing out her hair when the roar of a powerful car engine smashed through her consciousness — trampling the frayed straws she'd grasped at since unearthing the *kalthruth*.

As she peeked through the curtains at the window next to her dresser, she barely stopped herself from screaming. On the narrow street below, a lanky figure had slammed his car door shut and was scooting up her steep front steps.

"Blainy," she said, her breath catching in her chest. Aside from his spacey appearance, she wondered what scared her about seeing him. Was she afraid he'd ask her to run away with him, or afraid she'd accept?

Or was it the sense that Blainy was totally controlled by that Yarrow creep, the guy Vance and the new kid said was so dangerous? Callie Ann shivered at the memory of Yarrow, trying to grab her forearm — until she'd squirmed away and picked up a chair to ward him off. For a moment his fingers had brushed her wrist and in that instant she'd sensed the depth of his cruelty.

Can't let him know I'm here, thought Callie Ann, wishing she hadn't left her iPhone on the back seat of the car. Not that she had much faith in either of the two boys. Whatever, she had to act fast. Based on the little she'd understood of what Vance and the spazzy new kid were saying, there wasn't much time left to save Lena from ... whatever ... was coming.

"Callie Ann!" Blade yelled up from her front steps, as she let the curtain fall gently back into place.

Knowing Blade, Callie Ann realized, it wouldn't be long before he forced the door off its hinges and ran upstairs to get her. His habit of breaking the rules had been one of the things that attracted her to him. His impulsiveness had been ... exciting. Now, she saw, it was also a liability.

Think!

If it weren't for the tight bridesmaid gown she was wearing, she figured she could probably climb out through the window in her parents' bedroom. But showing up with her dress in tatters wasn't exactly an option. She'd be lucky to get within 20 feet of Lena before the adults would start asking questions.

Her only option was the storm cellar door that opened out into her backyard. She'd squeeze through the gap in the hedgerow and be out on Cherry Lane in a couple of minutes, then head over to the reception. She'd call Vance on Lena's cell when she got there — if they hadn't figured things out for themselves by then.

Down below, Blade Northrop's voice boomed as his fists pounded again and again on the front door. Good thing her parents had already gone ahead to the reception.

"Time to go," Callie Ann whispered. Having yanked off the matching sling back pumps her mom had insisted were a required part of the outfit, she clutched them to her left hip and raced downstairs to the cellar.

"Stupid shoes," she mumbled, thinking how much faster she could go in her Nikes. And what about when she hit the street? Reaching the basement, she grabbed a pair of her dad's fishing boots and shoved her feet into them at the last minute.

Having heaved open the storm cellar door, she climbed out and headed down Cherry Lane as fast as possible, the *squoosh, squoosh, squoosh* of her father's loose, rubbery boots making a goofy counterpoint to her throbbing heart. And as she rounded the corner onto Orchard Drive, she could still hear echoes of Blade's voice bellowing her name.

"Poor Blainy," she said, wiping her eyes with her free hand. What would happen to him? Then again, what would happen to everyone if dorky Derek's plan didn't work? Better not to think like that; better to just *run.*

CHAPTER FORTY

High above Callie Ann's storm door, aboard the *Kryldria Valaarn,* Captain Dahaleen Altriavahn darted down vast, cylindrical corridors on her way to the bridge. A seasoned interstellar pilot, she accepted the starspanner's zero-gee environment as a necessary evil. There was, after all, no practical fuel-to-mass ratio that would permit Snaldrialooran engineers to recreate the cozy slosh of the Homeworld.

Even given the instantaneous leaps they could achieve with quantum transfer engines, Snaldrialooran particle physicists, astrophysicists and flight engineers were forced to take mass into account. As they had learned through bitter experience, displacing too large a volume of space-time could have disastrous consequences — like hurling ship and crew into the swirling gravitational wake of a dark star.

Finding a solution had meant re-imagining the entire shipboard experience. Each crewmember was outfitted with a cocoon of dense, synthetic materials flexible enough to conform to the contours of their bodies, yet sturdy enough to contain their accustomed atmosphere — a fluid slurry that was 82% liquid methane. At zero-gee, with the proper training, crewmembers aboard the *Kryldria Valaarn* could propel themselves about the ship with their tentacles — in a close approximation of the swimming they took for granted back home.

As the decorated war hero rippled her body through the airless void of the ship, she ran through the probability matrix she'd glimpsed on the Galactic Array. No matter how she read the data, the problems posed by this supposedly routine police action were mounting exponentially.

Settling into the command station near the nose of the ship, Captain Altriavahn forced herself to confront the confusing sensor data her science officers had picked up from the surface of the alien planet below.

Considering the exquisite control of time and space her culture had achieved in the last 4,500 years, she marveled at how easily Snaldrialooran dominance could potentially be shattered by one rebellious boy. Even if most of the danger implied by sensor data didn't originate with Ixdahan, his treasonous act had still set a terrible war machine in motion.

Tapping the tips of her tentacles together, the captain found Ixdahan's criminal motivation depressingly clear. Aside from pure greed, the biases of his social class had allowed him to believe the Vrukaari were too barbaric to pose a meaningful threat.

Granted, the Vrukaari were a species of arrogant bunglers, but their incompetence was overshadowed by their ferocity. Was their violent nature the reason the Interstellar Consortium had recalled her from patrol duty in the sleepier sections of the Alychiataan sector? The captain shook her head. If she had been selected on the basis of her battle record — a series of brilliant tactical moves in the bloody Jahldrellian War — why had she been given only a single ship and the humiliating rank of Space Nanny?

Had the Snaldrialooran Synod decided to ignore the threat, or did contempt also blind them to the possibility that the Vrukaari could master transmog technology? Rolling her eyes, Captain Altriavahn realized either explanation was equally plausible.

With their ancient civilization and highly-evolved sense of moral responsibility, the august members of the Synod would never have imagined that the Vrukaari, eager to try out their new toys, would ignore standard safety protocols designed to protect their test subjects.

How appalled they would be to learn that the Vrukaari had achieved their rudimentary grasp of transmog theory through a brutal process of trial and error, resulting in the harsh disfigurement or sickening death of a thousand or more "volunteers."

"If the Synod had seen what I've seen...." said the captain out loud. But enough speculation! The situation on the ground was about to get ugly.

Now, according to the scanner data trickling in on her console, the Vrukaari were attempting the direct transference of embryonic cells into soldier-clones, fully adapted to this alien environment — and fully programmed for battle.

According to Dahaleen's science officers, it was a feat of transmog technology no one had tried before. Should she write this down to the enemy's foolish bravado, or had the Vrukaari received help from the Snaldrialooran exile? The data was muddy. On one hand, the DXN units sent to monitor the wayward boy had been offline for several rotations.

If the boy had the technical expertise to disable them on his own, might he also have the expertise to program the Vrukaari transmog units that would carry out this delicate operation?

No, it made no sense. Nothing in the boy's background suggested unusual prowess in anything beyond vanity, deception and theft. His data profile could be taken at face value. Ixdahan Daherek was a typical product of the Snaldrialooran "upper crust" — spoiled, avaricious, narcissistic and with no sense of duty to the Homeworld.

To think children like *this* grew up to attain the highest political offices. *Sacred Mentality of the Dark Voids!* How had the Homeworld survived the passage of time?

No, the captain decided.... Putting the boy at the center of the coming disaster would be a dangerous miscalculation. That kind of thinking would only repeat the mistake of her superiors: underestimate the Vrukaari and get caught unprepared.

"Not that I have many tactical options," she said to the tactical team standing by in a lander to retrieve Ixdahan. Her assignment was to recapture an escaped exile, not intervene in an intergalactic war. On the other hand, sending her tiny corps of, essentially, police officers into what would soon become a scene of horrific slaughter was not an acceptable risk.

Trouble was, failing to return with the son of the Honorable Pertahru Daherek was also not an option. It would mean the end of both her military career and her civil liberties. She could look forward to forced relocation to the third moon of Snaldrialoor Secunda — where she would live out her days tending herds of *grizalkianarh* at a state-sponsored farming collective.

Nodding her head, Captain Altriavahn recognized a familiar battlefield paradox: though this was no time for rash decisions, she nevertheless had to act quickly and decisively. With one ship, a limited array of weaponry and the sure knowledge she couldn't hide from Vrukaari sensors for much longer, she could hardly mount a major offensive. Her only hope was to find a weak spot in the enemy's battle plan and take ruthless advantage of it before the battle could even begin.

Scanning the mentallic fields below with the aid of the Galactic Array and the combined efforts of her mentalometric specialists, she now believed she had found that weakness. The discovery would have brought her great satisfaction, if it hadn't been shaded a moment later by a second discovery. The diplomat's son was attempting to disrupt the assault with the help of Earth children — one of whom had even managed to attain rudimentary mentallic awareness.

Impressive, as was the boy's attempt to mask his presence with a Class 1 scenario field. For now, he'd managed to convince the Vrukaari operative that his DXN units were still functioning normally — though his success had as much to do with Lieutenant Colonel Yarrow's ego, including his refusal to believe he could be outwitted by "a mere boy."

Eyes shut tight, the pragmatic starspanner captain slumped back in the command console couch and sighed. The slightest action on her part would only focus Yarrow's attention on the boy, ensuring his death.

And there it stood: Captain Altriavahn's years of military service, her brilliant tactical mind and the advanced technology she controlled were of no use to her in this situation. Her only course of action was to do *absolutely nothing* — and hope that in the confusion of the attack, her special ops team could gather up Ixdahan in time for her to slip away unnoticed.

As to the proto-stellar alien society beneath her, she wouldn't wager a handful of *kahthaljah* beans it would survive the week. It was useless to think ... but ... wait....

If a direct assault on the Vrukaari was impossible, perhaps she could still give the exile's plan a tiny nudge. Yes, Captain Altriavahn nodded, the procedure would be simple and unobtrusive. All she needed to accomplish was a sudden, critical cooling of the upper atmosphere plus a sufficient quantity of silver nitrate, frozen carbon dioxide and, perhaps, sodium chloride — a substance the humans referred to as "salt."

How long had it been, she wondered, since people on the Homeworld had referred to chemical compounds by other than their scientific names? 3,500 years? Unlucky Earth creatures: the universe had arrived on their doorstep at least a dozen centuries too early.

CHAPTER FORTY-ONE

Derek's mind nearly snapped with the combined stress of monitoring five different mental channels, while simultaneously tracking the Snaldrialooran lander and the Vrukaari *kalthruth* buried at Harmony Beach. By now, he and Vance had given up waiting for Callie Ann; they only hoped she'd sneaked past Blade and would soon reach the wedding reception.

Though it scared Derek to base his tactical decisions on such paper-thin logic, he had no other option. One glimpse of Derek and Vance in Callie Ann's car would have aroused Blade's rage — and caught the attention of Yarrow, who couldn't have been more than minutes away from initiating his assault on Earth.

On Derek's orders, Vance backed out of their spot behind the forsythia bush as quietly as possible, then took off in the direction of Derek's house.

"We gotta do something," grumbled Vance. "What if he finds her?"

"Just get me home," said Derek in a whisper as they rounded a corner. "I can use my robots' transponder to boost my mentallic fields and...."

Derek's throat went dry at the sight of 100 Blade clones meandering through the streets, tending to the random clumps of mailboxes that, by now, had sprung up everywhere.

"What are they...." Vance started to yell.

"It's the last phase before the assault," said Derek. "We have to get moving."

That's when Callie Ann's Corolla came to a halt.

"Out of gas," said Vance. "I told you...."

But Derek was already out of the car, racing up Chicory Lane toward his house.

Meanwhile, in the dank recesses of the ruined Skudderton post office, the Vrukaari military leader was hesitating. The sensor data from the Lander Team continued to contradict the data from the sensor array he'd installed in the Skudderton post office. Was the Snaldrialooran vessel responsible for the data drift or were the Earth creatures' crude electronics creating stray signals?

Enough! With the clarity of a battle-hardened mind, Lieutenant Colonel Relsheesharb Yarrow of the 123rd Regiment made a fateful decision. In a breach of Vrukaari protocol, he jumped up from the console, snatched the transponder gear off his head and leaped over to the nearest window.

"Atmospheric conditions normal," he growled at the clear blue sky above him. That settled it. He'd begin the assault without waiting for final confirmation from his clone-operatives on the eastern hemisphere. That was also against protocol, but he had to act before the Snaldrialoorans intervened. Now that his sensor array had become unreliable, who knew how many ships they had hidden behind this planet's huge moon?

As he strutted back to this command console, the only thing corroding the Lieutenant Colonel's resolve was the creaky gnash of bone, muscle and sinew that accompanied his every movement. There was no question that his time occupying this humanoid shell had dampened his spirits. So let him finish this tactical exercise, the first of its kind, then return to Vrukaar 4 with full honors — and restored to his former magnificence!

"Steady," he told himself. On second thought, it made no sense to strike before his forces were ready. Besides, the confirmation he needed was only minutes away and, he had to admit, he was working with equipment cobbled together too hastily to allow for proper alignment and testing. High Command had even taken the unusual step of sending him without a full support staff, so eager were Their Wisdoms to complete this test run. Instead, he had only the handful of sluggish technicians who made up the Lander Team.

Never mind. That was one more item to add to the detailed account he would file when he returned in triumph. His scathing report of how this mission had been mismanaged would be the leading edge of the military reforms he would institute immediately.

There! His eastern-hemisphere operatives had completed their final system checks. It was time to act ... but ... what had caused ambient light levels to drop so fast in the last few seconds and....

Yarrow's jaw dropped as a crack of thunder pounded out a terrifying roar in the near distance.

The electrical storm! It was coming after all, and at the worst possible time. Already, the first static electrical discharges were lighting up the horizon. If one of them struck the *kalthruth*....

Breathing heavily, Yarrow snatched up the transponder headgear he had discarded a moment ago and jammed it down over his temples. Now that the Lander Team's sensor array had proven accurate, he would initiate the final commands as planned, through the offshore transponder.

"Commence transmog sequence *Archilzarnach-Iz-Kalthruthianoor*," he said mentallically. "Transmog embryonic cells to...."

But despite his iron will, polished through decades of decisive military victory, the seasoned warrior was astonished to find he could not complete his thought. An external power source was jamming ... inter ... cept ... ing....

All around him was chaos, the electrical storm was mounting in intensity, the lightning strikes coming closer with each flash, the winds whipping up with brutal force. And there in the distance, an unexpected sound: a sports car engine, revved up to high gear, roaring directly through the collapsed outer walls of the post office!

CHAPTER FORTY-TWO

As she milled through the crowd of family and friends at the Sweet Harbor Inn, Lena's mind wandered back and forth through several streams of thought and memory. Dad's wedding was more beautiful than she'd expected, considering it had been pulled together in less than three weeks. Rhea's keen eye for design, which Lena had noticed for the first time in her floral arrangements, had tuned a frumpy tourist trap into a graceful, celebratory space.

Not even the persistent presence of fake-Mom could distract Lena from the satisfaction she read in Dad's eyes whenever he looked in her direction.

And yet, at a different level of consciousness, Lena scanned the edges of the mentallic field surrounding Skudderton for any signs of change. Was there a message for her out there, encoded in a puzzling phrase or cryptic image? It was too hard to tell at this distance and she dared not zoom in any closer — with fake-Mom hovering at the margins of her mind.

It didn't matter. By clearing her thoughts, Lena could sense the change that had come over the texture of the mentallic fields surrounding her. They were becoming "darker," "more intense" and "more intricate" — words borrowed from the physical world that conjured only a crude approximation of her senses.

Which of those changes reflected the actions of ... her friends ... and which were the result of ... others ... was impossible to tell.

"Look at you sulking by yourself," the disapproving voice of fake-Mom echoed through her thoughts. "Keep going and you'll make your father worried on his special day. Is that nice?"

"OK, this is seriously annoying," Lena muttered as she headed for the punch bowl, her soft leather pumps pounding ineffectively into the dining room's olive green, spill-resistant carpet. But no sooner did she realize the intensity of the anger rising in her chest than she stopped, turned around and walked slowly out to the Inn's side porch overlooking a quiet country road.

Breathing in the air, tinged with a faint scent of the ocean, Lena summoned her strength, calmed her raging emotions and resisted the urge to lash out against the increasingly life-like vision of ... of Mom.

"She was never like that," Lena whispered into a soothing breeze rising up to her from the east. And as her anger subsided, the vision began to fade along with it, now once again relegated to the extreme edge of her thoughts. The more she engaged with the hallucination, the more power it could have over her. And yet, how great it would be to sit down with Mom again over a cup of cocoa....

"That's enough," Lena said out-loud, and she forced herself to go back inside where the positive emotions of Dad's and Rhea's wedding reception would help her regain her equilibrium.

"So nice to see you rejoining the others," said fake-Mom, her voice now softer, gentler than a moment ago.

"Lena!" said Dad, coming up to her the moment she entered the main dining room. "Callie Ann has been looking for you for the last 20 minutes. Is everything...?"

"Callie Ann is *here*?" asked Lena, feeling dizzy. What was happening?

A deep rumbling welled up in the distance, intensifying until it seemed to make the ground shake beneath her. Thinking at first this was another hallucination, she tried to block the sensation out with her mind.

But as Lena gazed at the rest of the reception guests, their gowns and tuxedos ruffled by the wind, she realized the sound was real, tangible. A thunderstorm? But ... weird ... it was only raining in one part of town.

"Lena," said Callie Ann, tugging on her forearm.

"What are you...." Lena sputtered.

"I gotta ask you a question," said Callie Ann, taking Lena by the elbow. Before Lena could answer, fake-Mom appeared, looking more real, more solid, as she forced her way between Lena and Callie Ann.

"Stay away from that dirty girl," said fake-Mom, her fake eyes flaring wide.

"Lena." Callie Ann's voice cut through the thick mental fog encasing Lena's mind. "Answer me!"

"What did you...." Lena started to say, feeling as if her legs were collapsing under her.

" ... dessert," Callie Ann was screaming. "What's your favorite dessert?"

What a simple question, Lena reflected, her body floating effortlessly on the ocean at Felicity Bay. It was a question she could answer easily, if only it mattered.

"That's right, Lenaroo," fake-Mom's soothing voice sang out over the horizon. "Focus on what matters. Focus, focus, focus."

"Lena." A faint trace of Callie Ann's voice echoed in the distance, or was that the sound of sea gulls squawking overhead?

"I just heard from Silvano," the soaring birds continued. "He's coming back to America and wants to know what your favorite dessert is so he can surprise you. What should I tell him?"

"That's easy," said Lena. Her voice was quiet and serene, as the salt water closed itself gently over her, pulling her down. "It's lime Jell-O. Everybody knows I love lime Jell-O."

In an instant, people across town watched, jaws dropping, as a surge of green, gelatinous slime gushed out of the mutant mailboxes on every street corner and slid down into the sewer drains, little realizing this sight would soon be repeated across cities, towns and villages in every sector of the planet. Back in Skudderton, people on the street had even more to puzzle over, as a severe thunderstorm raged, curiously, over just one city block.

It was the block at the intersection of Trolley Lane and Poplar Road where, as local residents remembered for the first time in weeks, the post office had once stood, though it was now a tangled wreck of granite and steel.

Were they more astonished by the lightning strikes that had pummeled it repeatedly in the last half hour, or by the sight of a tall teenage boy ramming an expensive, gunmetal gray sports car right into the ruined hulk and smashing his way through to ... to what?

For the moment, in the reception hall at Sweet Harbor Inn, everyone's attention was on Lena, lying collapsed in what Dad, Rhea and their wedding guests assumed was a coma. But it was nothing of the kind; she was lost in a transient world between thought, matter, space and time — which she would never have perceived without coming in contact with the Vrukaari fungus.

Though it was the kind of experience Todd Gabrilowicz would hardly have called a "blessing," Lena found the eerie clarity of her mind deeply soothing. She could see, hear, feel everything, from the rustling of leaves down by Old Creek road, to the hum of high tension wires out on Route 72, to the sound of the wind chimes on her own front porch, the ones Aunt Kathy had brought down from Vancouver last fall.

Farther away, farther than seemed possible, Lena also heard the grim murmuring of commands given and taken on board the Snaldrialooran ship where, even now, Captain Altriavahn was discussing what to do with "the prisoner."

"At least he *did* something," said Lena, standing before a massive alien creature wrapped tight in a metallic encounter suit. "You should have listened to him," she added, trying to project an air of grave dignity, despite the tremble in her voice. At first, it seemed as if the huge, eight-tentacled creature hadn't heard her. But after a slight delay, the captain gave a startled glance in Lena's direction — and everything went black.

CHAPTER FORTY-THREE

Lena awoke in back of an ambulance, to the sight of Dad and Rhea looking down at her. Dad's eyes, red and puffy, lit up and a smile broke out on Rhea's face. Still in their wedding clothes, they looked so out of place in the ambulance that Lena would have giggled if her mouth hadn't been so dry.

"You'll miss your honeymoon," Lena croaked through parched lips, before dozing off.

A few days later at twilight, after a brief hospital stay, Lena looked out on the world from her back porch and found serious joy in breathing the crisp evening air. It was as fresh and beautiful as she could have wished for, but that couldn't compare to the satisfaction of thinking clearly again.

Gone were the buzzing, humming, laughing, murmuring crowd sounds of the last few weeks. They had left behind a pristine silence against which only her thoughts echoed.

Also gone was the excitable glow of Derek's hyperactive mind. Though Lena knew she'd miss the indescribable sensation of telepathic communication, she relished the idea of being alone, private, secure in her own mind.

"Must have been freaky," she'd heard Vance say by cell phone an hour before. "I mean, seeing inside people's heads and all. By the way," he added in a low voice, "you didn't do any, you know, snooping...."

"Like it would take a mind reader to know what *you* think about every second," said Lena with a laugh. "Besides, half the time I had those 'amazing superpowers' I couldn't even use them."

"Good thing Dude kept it together, then." said Vance. "You seen Alien Boy around lately?"

But Lena hadn't. Derek had vanished soon after the first reports that the mysterious mutant mailboxes were disappearing around the world.

Earth was getting back to normal. In fact, work on repairing the Skudderton post office had stopped almost as soon as it started.

"Check it, it's like, healing itself," said Vance.

Even Blade Northrop's car had vanished, melted into a pool of gray, metallic sludge the moment the mailboxes started spewing lime Jell-O. That is, the nearest approximation to Jell-O the Vrukaari transmog device could manage once it received Lena's mentallic command.

That piece of news was a tough break for Callie Ann — who had never given up hope for her "Blainy." Lena knew better than to try to comfort her with words. The most she could do was hang out with Callie Ann, to be there whenever she needed her best friend.

"Takes a long time to get over a loss like that," Rhea had said at dinner.

Bad enough when everything's normal, thought Lena, remembering how she'd felt when Dad had told her about Mom.

The next morning, before rushing off to school, she got an IM from Silvano, whose Dad was getting ready to move back to the States.

> Monsters gone away.
> Monster comin' home
> 2 monster U =]

It would be good to see Silvano again, and maybe kind of weird. After months of having Derek in her life ... but then, who had Derek been to her? Well ... for starters, he'd been in her mind, he'd seen her thoughts and communicated with her in a more intimate way than anyone else could. So was she wrong to let him go now?

It's not like you have a choice, she heard Derek's voice sound in her mind.

"You...." Lena said aloud. "What happened to you?"

Meet me at the lockers, Derek's voice echoed. *I'll try to explain.*

After what felt like the slowest school bus ride in history, Lena rushed through the front doors of her school and over to the lockers where an eerie quiet lingered in the air. Lena's eyes widened at the sight of students standing as still as the mannequins at the Skudderton-Thornberry Mall.

"I wanted to say goodbye," said Derek, coming around the corner from a shiny glass trophy cabinet Lena had never noticed before. "But not in front of everybody."

"What did you ... did you stop time?" asked Lena.

"Don't worry," said Derek. "It isn't permanent."

"Not too much is," said Lena, looking down at her Adidas. "I'll never see you again."

"Doesn't look good," said Derek, resting his hands on Lena's shoulders. "But I can give you a choice that might increase the odds — if it matters enough to you."

"What kind of...." Lena started, her throat too dry to continue.

"My Homeworld is getting ready to disrupt biologic and digital memory across the entire planet," said Derek. "It's the only way to keep your societies from collapsing."

"Why?" asked Lena. "Can't we just ... get used to the idea that we're not alone?"

"I don't understand it, either," said Derek, "but it's something about the way our presence clashes with your belief systems ... our experts think it would take away the whole basis of your cultures and give you nothing to replace it."

"But you could stay, right?" Lena asked. "Explain things, teach us?"

"And what would you be, then?" asked Derek, staring straight into her eyes, "Pets?"

As Derek explained, the memory of the last few months would be replaced with implanted memories, a feat of mind control the Snaldrialoorans had tried only once before in their history. Lena smiled at the clear sense of pride Derek took in describing the plan. But confronted with her question about Blade, Derek hung his head.

"It will be as if ... when his car crashed outside of Harmony Beach ... it was a simple case of DWI."

"You mean you can erase billions of memories in a couple of hours?" asked Lena.

"Minds are malleable. And, anyway, we won't be erasing anything. Just rewriting," said Derek.

"But...." Lena started.

"I can't explain it any better," said Derek. "At least not now. I want to make sure you have time to make your decision."

"What decision?" asked Lena, looking him deep in the eyes. "You want me to go with you?"

"Yes ... but ... you can't," said Derek rubbing the back of his neck. "I need you to make a different decision. I made my Homeworld promise to let you remember ... me, everything, if you choose. You'd be the only one, but after everything we put you through — that I put you through — I told them they owed you."

"You *made* them promise?" asked Lena, squinting at him.

"I invoked *khaldahrn drolghar* — personal preference," said Derek. "Even criminals have rights, you know."

"No, I wouldn't know," said Lena. "I've never been in your kind of trouble."

"So does ... does that mean you'd rather forget?" asked Derek, his face going pale.

"I totally want to remember you," said Lena. "And I want you to remember this," she added, leaning in to kiss him on the lips.

A second later, Derek was gone, snatched up in mid-sentence as technicians from his Homeworld reassigned his quantum signature to match the coordinates of the Snaldrialooran starspanner parked on the far side of Earth's pock-marked moon.

For a brief moment, Lena was alone, suspended in time between a world with Derek and a world without even his memory. But before she could blink twice more, the locker room burst into life again, with every ounce of teenage energy ricocheting off the brightly colored walls.

From then on, whenever Lena would remember this time in her life, a time she alone had the privilege to remember, her mind would always focus first on Derek's final words to her.

"I'll send you a postcard," he'd said, as a sly smile crept up his face, "from the Crab Nebula. Thanks for the...."

For what, she'd always wonder: For her fashion tips, for believing in him — or for his "first contact" with a formerly telepathic Earth girl?

CHAPTER FORTY-FOUR

Millions of miles from the lockers at Skudderton High, the navigational systems aboard *Kryldria Valaarn* were preparing to make the first spatio-temporal leap on their journey home. Encased in a translucent environment sphere programmed to support his human body, Ixdahan was completely cut off from Captain Altriavahn and her crew.

In fact, for the first two days of his journey, his only visitors had been the robotic dining cart and the robotic cleaning unit that rolled in once every twelve hours to sweep, mop and sanitize. For the first time in his life, he was totally alone with his thoughts; the environment sphere blocked mentallic access to anyone on board and even prevented him from connecting to the Galactic Array.

So now, added to his many regrets was his inability to contact his cousin Jalgren Altrollinhar, the only family member he'd had any contact with since he left the Homeworld.

"It's my own fault," he said into his hands, which at the moment were clasped tight over his eyes. In a frantic grab for cash, he'd endangered the lives of an entire population and upset the balance of power in his home galaxy.

Worse, the consequences of his actions might not be known for several rotations. No one on the Homeworld or any of the Associated Cultures had studied the impact of mentallic control on a planetary scale. How far had they disrupted human history and what impact would the subtlest residue of their mentallic field have on the future of human evolution?

"Not that there was any other option," said Captain Altriavahn when Ixdahan had first arrived on board. "Nice work. As catastrophes go, this could have been worse — you thought fast and pulled together a plan. Of course, you had an advantage: You started this mess."

And, in case anyone should forget, the Vrukaari, as the starspanner captain had made a point of telling Ixdahan, were already boasting of the progress they'd made in the design and manufacture of transmog technology. Though they had suffered a humiliating defeat on

Earth, they would live to fight again — this time with full control of a game-changing weapon of mass destruction.

The fate of two galaxies would never be the same — just because he'd been too desperate for spending money, the gleaming credit tiles that could transmog a powerless, laughable and dorky boy into a charismatic, fashionable, sexy beast.

"I had all that," he whispered into the darkness surrounding him. "Well, maybe not the sexy part," he added, thinking back at the telling smirk he'd seen on Edahen Tricebehat's face when he'd asked her out for dinner. Even so, there were other girls he could have had a chance with — except for the whole egomaniac thing he had going on.

It wasn't the lack of money, he saw now, that had driven him to steal. Nor had he acted solely out of anger when Father had cut his allowance. It was the longing for respect he believed he'd never earn while living in the shadow of the Homeworld's most distinguished politician.

Yet for a short time he *had* found respect among the hideous Earth creatures he'd finally become accustomed to.

"I miss them," he told himself, his stomach tightening. Without the vaunted mentallic accomplishments of his species, without a true space-faring culture, or even tentacles, Lena, Vance, and crabby Callie Ann had taken him in, taken him seriously and stood by him. They'd stood by him even when they had every right to hate him for what he'd done.

So as the miserable, lonely hours passed, Ixdahan made up his mind. Even if he were sent to prison, he'd take every opportunity to make something useful out of himself. He'd never forget Yarrow's cruelty, experienced firsthand and mind-to-mind, during his brief, superficial scan of his consciousness.

Back on Earth, Lena awoke to a typical day in Skudderton, on the most atypical day in human history: The first day humanity had lived with altered memory — everyone except her, that is. On the other hand, if her own memories had been tampered with, how would she have known? Had Derek given her a choice to remember, or had he chosen for her?

"No way to tell," she said as she gazed out at the sunrise brightening her windows and spilling out slowly into her room. Besides, she realized, she had more immediate puzzles to solve, like making it through Junior Year, applying to college — and getting used to sharing

Dad with Rhea. As grateful as Lena was for Rhea's warmth, sympathy and common sense, it still wasn't easy to see her coming out of Dad's bedroom in the morning.

But, OK, stuff happens and you have to be prepared. What? Was Lena really going to say Rhea was more "alien" than Derek or ... geez ... the Vrukaari?

"Get real," she mumbled, as she rummaged around in her dresser for underwear. Besides, she realized, she had to focus on preparing herself: Silvano would be back in town by the end of next week. What would it be like to see him again in person? And how would she feel, knowing she could never tell him about the most fascinating experience of her life?

Never mind about that, Lena decided. She'd have to make her life interesting in other ways, so she could share *those* experiences with sweet Silvano instead. No way she could let the last two months be the only thing memorable about her. There was more to Lena Gabrilowicz than strange little Derek.

Not that she had any regrets. Her experience with Derek had opened her mind to a new way of thinking. Even without the mentallic senses she'd known only briefly, she now had a vision of the wider universe and a new way to see herself.

School? Dad? Metalwork? Biology? Boyfriends? Probably easier to handle than an alien invasion. Well, she'd never want to see Dad and Silvano as "easy." And her interest in art and science was real. But now Lena knew she had no reason to doubt herself.

The only thing left to trouble her was the memory of Mom. But Lena's contact with Derek had changed that, too. Seeing the hallucination Yarrow had planted in her head had put that memory in perspective.

"I know everything I need to remember about her," Lena whispered as she pulled on her jeans. And in that moment she felt the freedom to let go of Mom's memory, the courage to live without hugging it tight like the fuzzy brown teddy bear Dad bought her in Atlantic City the summer she was four. As the Vrukaari soldier had shown her with blunt realism, Mom's place in Lena's heart was forever.

CHAPTER FORTY-FIVE

"Wake up," snarled a voice in Ixdahan's mind, at what would have been the wee hours of the morning on Earth. The voice was the first trace of mentallic contact Ixdahan had felt since leaving Earth and it hit him like a splash of ice water.

"Father?" Ixdahan asked, shielding his thoughts with a standard privacy screen as fast as possible.

"Listen carefully," said Pertahru Daherek, Senior Ambassador to the August Assembly of Inner Worlds. "The next mind you connect with belongs to Chaldraheen Ishialdrol. Do you know who that is?"

"Group Leader, Intergalactic Security, Khaltreaballoorn Sector" Ixdahan replied, his mentallic field trembling. "Father, I...."

"Don't interrupt," said Pertahru. "It will be more rotations than I have left before you'll earn back the right to do that. Understood?"

"Yes, Sir," said Ixdahan, wishing he were sitting across from Lena and Vance again in the cafeteria at Skudderton High.

"Now, I've gone to a lot of trouble to broker you a deal with Group Leader Ishialdrol," said Pertahru, "and I advise you to take it. People like you don't get many chances to set things right."

"People like me?" said Ixdahan, feeling his human chest tighten. If he needed any reminder of why he'd dealt with the Vrukaari, this was it. But Pertahru was right, even if admitting defeat *did* bring his dinner dangerously close to his throat.

"I wonder what Mother would say...." Ixdahan started.

"Your mother has suffered enough, because of you," snapped Pertahru, "yet even now she begs me to give you her greetings."

"Mother?" said Ixdahan, trying to make contact, but was saddened to perceive the intricate mentallic barriers that shielded Pertahru's thoughts.

"Ishialdrol is coming through now," said Pertahru, his voice rimed with icy indifference. "Listen and make your decision. If you accept his terms, in 10 or 15 cycles ... I *might* be able to persuade the Consortium to grant you a pardon."

"And then?" asked Ixdahan, feeling as if his life were being snatched from under his nose by a greedy rodent.

But Pertahru was gone. In his place, was the calm civility of Group Leader Ishialdrol. As head of security for the third largest sector of the Near Regions, Chaldraheen had seen far worse than a teenage boy with a talent for thievery, code hacking and irritating his father.

More to the point, from Ixdahan's perspective, was what the Group Leader proposed.

"It would be different this time," said Chaldraheen, "as an agent of the security team, you'd have much more freedom, a reasonable expense account and no robotic supervision."

"Sounds dangerous," said Ixdahan, his heart racing.

The Group Leader, encased like the ship's captain and crew in a sheath of protective shipwear, chuckled into his second left tentacle.

"You can bet it's safer than a cell block in the Hlachianoar asteroid belt," he said. "The guards there have too much time on their hands and little to turn to besides the prisoners for ... entertainment."

"You're talking about more sessions in the transmog chamber," said Ixdahan, remembering his painful experiences on his way on Earth.

But as the even-tempered security chief pointed out, Ixdahan could hardly hope to infiltrate Vrukaari High Command looking like an ape-descended Earth mammal. For that was the deal Pertahru had brokered for his wayward heir. In exchange for several years' service in a Snaldrialooran espionage unit, Ixdahan could have his freedom.

"Why would you trust me now," asked Ixdahan, "after what I ... I did?"

"Not for what you did," said Chaldraheen, "for what you undid." As the Group Leader explained, there were people in Central Security who still denied Ixdahan could have defeated Yarrow acting alone.

"I didn't act alone," Ixdahan insisted. "the humans...."

Ixdahan paused, sensing a subtle shift in Group Leader Ishialdrol's mentallic field.

"Let me give you a word of advice," Chaldraheen said. "If you agree to join us, don't bother to mention your preposterous conviction that the humans are anything more than *phytral-drenarhl.* No one will believe you."

"You think I'm lying," said Ixdahan, shoving his jaw forward, "why not throw me back in jail?"

"Because it's the best way I know to find out what really happened on 'Earth,'" said Group Leader Ishialdrol. "It's rough out there in the field," he added. "Sooner or later, if you have any special connections to the criminal world, you'll have to use them to survive. And when you do, we'll finally have the opening we need to convict them. You follow?"

"But I'm telling the...." Ixdahan said. He never got to finish. The Group Leader had closed contact, leaving Ixdahan with a stark choice.

Hours later, the once-Snaldrialooran-once-human son of a haughty diplomat found himself tucked into a polished, late-model transmog chamber onboard a Central Security transport. As he lapsed into the first of several comas he'd have to endure, he heard a familiar voice nearby.

"Stay in contact," said Captain Altriavahn, her massive frame leaning over to get his attention. "I saw what you did down there. I know what you were up against. For a soft-willed hedonist you handled yourself well. I'm sending you my contact frequencies now."

"You don't want to get mixed up in my ... trouble," murmured Ixdahan with whatever was left of his human mouth.

"I already am," she said, twisting her tentacles together. "I'll be on patrol duty for at least another three cycles for exceeding my orders, but don't let that worry you. Need anything, just send out the frequencies. Only this time...."

"Yes?" asked Ixdahan as the atmosphere in his chamber was gradually replaced with chlorine gas.

"Try to make your request less planetary," the captain replied.

Hours later, in the midst of a deep sleep, his mind now fully encoded into the Galactic Array for safe keeping, Ixdahan had an extraordinary dream. He was back on Earth, but in his Snaldrialooran body. Lena and Vance were there and the three of them were laughing their heads off.

Lying in front of them was Gary Reynolds, sprawled out like a stuffed turkey — having just tripped over all eight of Ixdahan's tentacles, each one encased in an identical blue gray Nike sneaker. No one, he knew, on any of the worlds he would ever encounter, would be able to appreciate that moment. And that left him no choice.

If it took forever, he'd return to Skudderton to tell Lena the whole story. His experiences on the primitive planet of gas breathers had given him what he'd never known on the Homeworld: friendship, compassion and trust. So no matter how many times the transmog chamber wracked his body with transgenomic remapping protocols, one thing would never change — he'd always have a heart of Earth.

THE END
OF THE FIRST BOOK IN

the CHANGING HEARTS OF IXDAHAN
DAHEREK

AUTHOR'S NOTE

HEART OF EARTH began with a vivid memory: that being a teenager on Earth was the worst punishment in the universe. So, having sealed the fate of the youngest intergalactic criminal on record, it seemed only natural to give him the harshest sentence imaginable.

"Transmogged" into a human teenager, Ixdahan Daherek has plenty of time to repent and learn about empathy from the primitives around him — before an act of interstellar terror threatens everything he loves about his planet of exile.

Like me, back in the day, Ixdahan learns more when he's out in the universe than he ever would sitting at home in his pajamas. For setting that example, my fine tentacled friend, the people of Earth are eternally grateful.

And if you enjoyed my story, remember that Chickadee Prince Books, the publisher who brought this to you, is a small independent artists' collective press devoted only to quality work, and it needs your word of mouth to survive. Please tell a friend and write a review on Amazon and Goodreads.

Mark Laporta, October 2014

"I'm *telling* you," said an insistent voice, "they developed it on their own!"

"Do you hear yourself?" asked an irritable voice. "The Vrukaari. Acquired. Magclad Tech. Without. Stealing It."

"Saw the prototype myself," said the insistent voice. "Made the blast from a particle rifle fan out like the tailfins of a Cahlneera blowfish."

"No need for vulgarity," said the irritable voice, with a slight tremor.

"You think that's gross," the insistent voice continued, "how about this? The cladding was dense enough to act as the hull of a starspanner."

"You saw *that*?" asked the irritable voice, belonging to Chaldraheen Ishialdrol, Group Leader, Intergalactic Security, Khaltreaballoorn Sector.

And so the excited mentallic conversation continued, across the 4.25 light years separating Snaldrialoor and Vrukaar Prime, until the insistent voice of FieldOp 2nd Class Ixdahan Daherek faded out into the emptiness of space-time.

Ixdahan shook his head. It was almost a year since his return from exile on Earth. Here he had defeated Lieutenant Colonel Relsheesharb Yarrow — and he still had to fight hard to be heard.

Really. His victory *should* have been enough to commute his sentence for treason. Did the classified files he sold Ambassador Ghaar lead straight to the invasion of Earth? Totally beside the point.

"Ungrateful *pilaarni*," mumbled Ixdahan, grinding his teeth. For it was only the influence of Pertahru, Ixdahan's father and Snaldrialoor's most distinguished diplomat, that had earned him this sliver of mercy: No jail time, in exchange for service in the Snaldrialooran Security Agency, referred to across the Seven Known Galaxies as the SSA.

Good thing no one on the Homeworld believed the "Earth creatures" had helped him stop the Vrukaari invasion, he realized. The more he captured the world's imagination as a hero acting alone, the higher his standing might rise — if he could ever live down betraying his people.

Of course, cousin Jalgren Altrollinhar, Professor of Transgenomics at Lohar University, also deserved some credit. He'd outlined the attack strategy Ixdahan had launched with his human friends, Lena, Vance and Callie Ann. But the last thing cousin Jalgren needed was a reputation for aiding intergalactic criminals.

And knocking down Ixdahan's heroic myth another notch was the last minute assist he'd received from Captain Dahaleen Altriavahn, the decorated commander of the Snaldrialooran starspanner, *Kryldria Valaarn.*

Those limitations aside, he knew he'd still been given a rare gift: The chance to show the universe he was just as brave as he was stupid — an opportunity most people would kill for.

"So glad that's over," said Ixdahan, stepping out onto the main plaza of Gitraarinahol, the capital city of Vrukaar Prime. It was time to make his rounds, undercover, as a Deputy Building Inspector.

It was also time to admit, as he had every day since emerging from the transmog chamber on an SSA starspanner, how disgusting it was to inhabit a Vrukaari body.

"Like living inside a rotting double-cheese pizza," he said to his robot assistant, 17/Chaarnactral.

"So you have told me," said the AI, its composite surface glinting slightly in the pale red light of Vrukaar Prime's dwarf star. "Though I find no mention of *pizza* or *cheese* on the Galactic Array."

"Skip it," said Ixdahan. "Just tell me where-to next."

It hardly mattered: His building inspections were as routine as they were futile. The Vrukaari real estate industry was so corrupt, he could cite a property owner with 100 major violations and no action would be taken — with the possible exception of bribery.

Besides, his real job was being the eyes and ears of the SSA in this sector of the city. His mission? To sniff out irregularities and alert Group Leader Ishialdrol to any unusual activity.

Up until last night, Ixdahan's posting had been as uneventful as the life cycle of a Jubthorian mud worm. He'd kept his senses open, filed his field reports and made an effort to take part in Vrukaari society — by making friends, turning up at the holotheatres and being seen out on the town with, occasionally, a female on his arm.

Not that the thought of making out — as one slab of rotting double cheese pizza to another — actually thrilled him. On the other hand, after a nearly a year of living each day as a Vrukaari, with Vrukaari senses and a Vrukaari set of appetites, he did occasionally find the prospect somewhat … mandatory.

"You're doing it again," said 17/Chaarnactral.

"Doing what?" asked Ixdahan, looking over at the robot as they exited the plaza and turned right onto Ghaltraxaan Boulevard.

"Shuddering," said the robot. "This is not a high probability behavior among your adopted people and will make you stand out."

"I'll keep that in mind," grunted Ixdahan. "Are we almost there?" he added, gazing at the squat, ovoid buildings that passed for office towers in this city.

Lena. Lena Gabrilowicz would understand, Ixdahan realized, remembering the Earth girl who had helped him take down the Vrukaari strike force leader. *She* knew what a double cheese pizza was. *She* knew what the expression "totally gross" meant, in a way neither his haughty Snaldrialooran countrymen nor the slime-drooling idiots he dealt with on Vrukaar Prime could grasp.

She was, in fact, the one person who understood *anything* about him — which was why, naturally, she lived thousands of parsecs away on a planet in the Remote Regions.

Not that his feelings weren't mixed on the subject of where he'd rather be.

As unpleasant as his life was on Vrukaar Prime, at least he was dealing with a mentallic people who were aware of the larger universe. Like it or not, it was easier to be himself in this galaxy — simply because the dominant cultures here were way more similar to the world he'd grown up with. And yet, on Earth, he'd found....

But, OK, this was no time to relive the past. If he were ever to return to a normal life on the Homeworld, he'd have to *deliver*. And that's why he'd been so excited to tell Group Leader Ishialdrol about the demonstration he'd seen last night at Shelsgriadahr University.

It was also why he was now so depressed that his report generated no enthusiasm.

"We'll look into it, FieldOp Daherek," Ishialdrol had said. "Good work, nice initiative. But we at the Bureau don't have the luxury of jumping to conclusions. Besides, none of our other operatives in Vrukaari space have reported anything similar."

"But...." Ixdahan sputtered.

"They're good people, Son, with a lot more field experience than you — and they can't corroborate your story. So it's possible your reading of the data is … imprecise. See my problem here? But go ahead, gather more evidence and we'll see where it leads."

At that rate, Ixdahan knew, the Vrukaari could develop The Ultimate Weapon before "the Bureau" so much as raised an eyebrow. Not that any of the blue-gray, eight-tentacled, liquid- methane-breathing Snaldrialooran security operatives actually had eyebrows.

"Raising an eyebrow," was an Earth expression from of one its many languages, an expression like countless others that had permanently altered his view of the universe.

www.ingramcontent.com/pod-product-compliance
Lightning Source LLC
Chambersburg PA
CBHW070026120726
47909CB00003B/1068